Whatever Happened to Janie?

Also by CAROLINE B. COONEY:

The Face on the Milk Carton
Twenty Pageants Later
Among Friends
Camp Girl-Meets-Boy
Camp Reunion
Family Reunion
The Girl Who Invented Romance
Operation: Homefront
Driver's Ed
Both Sides of Time

Whatever Happened to Janie?

CAROLINE B. COONEY

Delacorte
Press

Published by
Delacorte Press
Bantam Doubleday Dell Publishing Group, Inc.
1540 Broadway
New York, New York 10036

Library of Congress Cataloging in Publication Data

Cooney, Caroline B.
Whatever happened to Janie? / by Caroline B. Cooney.
p.   cm.
Summary: The members of two families have their lives disrupted
when a teenage girl who had been kidnapped twelve years earlier
discovers that the people who raised her are not her biological parents.
Sequel to The Face on the Milk Carton.
ISBN 0-385-31035-8
[1. Kidnapping—Fiction.   2. Parent and child—Fiction.   3. Brothers
and sisters—Fiction.   4. Identity—Fiction.]
I. Title
PZ7.C7834Wh   1993
[Fic]—dc20   92-32334
                                                         CIP
                                                          AC

Manufactured in the United States of America

June 1993

10   9   8   7

BVG

For Sayre,
who knew what happened to Janie

CHAPTER
1

After their sister's kidnapping, Dad not only took Stephen and Jodie to school every morning, he held their hands.

Not once—not once in a hundred and eighty days a year, kindergarten through sixth grade— were the remaining Spring children allowed to take a school bus. Not once had Jodie been allowed to walk in or out of the elementary school without her father there.

The children would get out of the car. Dad would take Jodie's hand in his right hand and Stephen's hand in his left. Then they would walk across the parking lot, into the building and down to Jodie's classroom where he would transfer Jodie's hand to the teacher's. His eyes would scan the halls, as if kidnappers were lurking beside the winning poster from the science contest. When Jodie was safely in her teacher's care, Dad would continue on with Stephen.

For years, Jodie thought this pattern was normal.

But when Stephen was in fourth grade, he said

if anybody ever held his hand again, he would bite it. He said if anybody had planned to kidnap another Spring child, they had given up by now. Stephen said he would carry a knife, he would carry a submachine gun, he would carry a nuclear bomb, and he would blow away all would-be kidnappers, but never again would he let anybody hold his hand.

From his fourth-grade heart had come the hidden rage they all felt and never dared say out loud.

"I hate Jennie!" Stephen had screamed. "I hate my sister for ruining our lives! The least Jennie could have done was leave her body there for us to find. Then we could bury her and be done with her. I hate it that we have to worry every single day. I hate her!"

Stephen was seventeen now. Jodie could remember that meal as if it were yesterday. Mom and Dad had sat as tight and silent as wind-up dolls. More vividly than anything else, Jodie remembered that nobody yelled at Stephen for saying such terrible things.

Years of worry had torn the family's guts apart, like a tornado peeling the house walls away. Worry had separated them from each other, so they were not six people knit close in tight, warm threads of family, but travelers accidentally in the same motel.

There had been a long, long silence after Stephen's outburst. Even the twins, who had been thick and annoying all their paired lives, knew better than to speak.

At last Dad had extended his hands from his

sides, straight out, like a Roman slave being crucified.

The whole family held hands every evening to say grace before supper. That was what Dad intended, and yet the stiffness of his arms, the awful lines around his mouth, did not look like grace.

Jodie had been scared, because she was between Dad and Stephen, and she would have to take Stephen's hand, and she was pretty sure Stephen really would bite her.

But he didn't.

He cried instead. Stephen had cried easily when he was little and the humiliation of that had left its mark; nothing would have made Stephen Spring cry now that he was seventeen. Where a ten-year-old had exhibited tears, the young man used fists.

So they had held hands, and Dad had prayed. Not grace. He didn't mention food. He didn't mention shelter. He said, "Dear Lord, tonight we are going to bury Jennie. We love her, but she's gone and now we're going to say good-bye. Thank you for the time we had Jennie. The rest of us have to go on living. Thank you for making Stephen tell us."

Jodie was only nine. Only a third-grader. Jodie had needed to take her hands back from Stephen and Daddy so she could wipe away her tears, and Jodie never admitted to anybody that they were not tears of grief for her missing sister, but tears of relief that they were going to put Jennie on the shelf and be done with her.

"Give Jennie a guardian angel," said Dad softly to the Lord.

Usually during grace, Jodie felt that Dad was

3

talking to his children, ordering them to behave and be thankful. Not this prayer. Dad was talking to the Lord; Jodie thought if she looked up she would see God, and that was even scarier than having to hold Stephen's hand, so she didn't look up.

"Take care of Jennie, Lord, wherever she is. Help us not mention Jennie again. Help us be a family of six and forget that we were ever a family of seven." Dad squeezed Jodie's hand.

Jodie squeezed Stephen's.

The squeeze went around the circle, and the Lord must have been there, because the lump in Jodie's throat dissolved, and the twins began to talk about sports—even when they were babies they talked about sports, they had been playing with basketballs and footballs and tennis balls from birth—and Stephen showed his B-plus geography paper; he had gotten forty-two of the fifty state capitals right.

The family sealed up, like a perfect package. Things fit again. Everything from the number of chairs around the table to the toppling stacks of presents under the Christmas tree. The Spring family had six people in it now. The seventh was gone.

Mom and Dad didn't even telephone Mr. Mollison again. Mr. Mollison was the FBI agent who had been in charge of the case. For a while he had been as much a part of the family as Uncle Paul and Aunt Luellen.

The next year, nobody talked about Jennie on her birthday. Nobody sobbed on the anniversary of the day Jennie went missing.

Mr. and Mrs. Spring were still more careful

4

than any other parents in the state of New Jersey, but the children were more careful, too. It was not because Jodie and her brothers were worried that they might be kidnapped, too. They were worried that their parents would be worried. The Spring children were always lined up at telephones to let Mom or Dad know where they were. They were never late. They were children who knew, too well, one of the horrors of the world.

The thing Jodie could not get over, now that her sister Jennie turned out to be alive and coming home, was that *there had never been a horror.*

They had imagined all of it.

Jennie had not died.

She had not been tortured.

She had not been cold or lost or drowned or raped or even frightened!

Jennie had been just fine all along.

It was incredible, when Jodie thought of the lancing fear the rest of them had endured for eleven and a half years. In most ways, of course, worry and fear vanished. When she was small, it vanished because Jodie believed in Daddy's deal with God. If Daddy and the Lord both said Stop Worrying, well then, who was Jodie to worry? But as Jodie moved into her teens, the reality of her sister's kidnapping often surfaced. When she brought a library book home . . . and the heroine was a redhead named Jennie. When Stephen had his first date . . . and her name was Jennie. When the late movie on television was about a kidnapping. When Jodie went in the post office and saw those black-and-white photos—HAVE YOU SEEN THIS CHILD?

5

She'd feel it again. The panic like burning acid, making it impossible to think of anything else. And the rage: the terrible, terrible anger that their lives had been so brutally interfered with.

Brian and Brendan were babies when it happened, still sitting in the double stroller, getting everything sticky. (Jodie's relationship with her twin brothers began by steering around them lest they smear her with melting lollipop or contaminate her with Oreo-cookie crumbs. Somehow it had continued that way. Keeping clear was Jodie's major activity with her little brothers.) But Jodie had been in kindergarten and Stephen in first grade, old enough to have memories, old enough to understand what had happened.

Well, no.

Not quite. Nobody had ever known what happened that day at the shopping mall. Nobody had ever known where Jennie was taken, or who took her, or for what purpose.

But all too well Jodie understood what happened to her family because of it.

It was so confusing and astonishing to find that all along, Jennie had been happy and healthy and warm and everything else that was good. The Springs had never needed to worry.

Mom and Dad were weak with relief and joy.

Jodie mentally laid her history of nightmares out on the bed, like laundry to be put away, and studied them, understanding less than ever.

Stephen, of course, was angry. Stephen didn't even have a fuse; he just continually exploded. Stephen yelled that Jennie ought to have suffered, since the rest of them had.

"Don't talk like that once she comes," warned their father. Dad was wildly excited. He and Mom kept bursting into shouts of laughter and hugging each other and hyperventilating. That was Jodie's new word—hyperventilate. Jodie did not want her family getting overly emotional, or too noisy. She felt it was time to drop the hand-holding at dinner and the saying of grace. Jennie would think they were weird. "Don't hyperventilate," Jodie begged constantly. But her family was the hyperventilating kind.

When Mom thought nobody was watching, she would rearrange the dining table, seeing where the seventh chair fit best. The chair her missing daughter would sit in when she came home. Then Mom would do a little tap dance around the chair, fingertips on the wood. She looked so comic, a forty-three-year-old, getting heavy, going gray, wearing sneakers that squeaked on the linoleum instead of tapping.

"We'll all have to work hard," Mom warned every night. "Jennie's grown up with another family. Different values, I suppose. This won't be easy." Mom burst into laughter, not believing a word of it. This was her baby girl. It would be easy and joyful. "We may have a hard time adjusting," she added.

This was for Stephen's benefit. Stephen was not a great adjuster.

Jodie planned to be the buffer between Jennie and Stephen. Jodie knew that she would not have problems. This was the sister with the matching J name. They would be like twins.

Brian and Brendan never noticed much of anything except each other and their own lives. Jodie thought it was such a neat way to live, wrapped up and enclosed with this secret best friend who went with you everywhere and was part of you.

That was how she would be with Jennie.

At night, when they were each in their own beds, with only a thin little table and a narrow white telephone to separate them, they would tell each other sister things. Jennie would tell Jodie details about the kidnapping that she had never told anybody. And Jodie would share the secrets of her life: aches and hurts and loves and delights she had never managed to confess to Nicole or Caitlin.

Jodie was cleaning her bedroom as it had never been cleaned before. Nicole and Caitlin said it was impossible to share a room this small. Two beds had been squeezed in, one tall bureau and one medium desk. Another person could never fit in her share of sweaters, earrings, cassettes, and shoes. Jodie was seized with a frenzy of energy, folding and refolding her clothing until it took up only half the space it used to; discarding left and right; putting paper grocery bags stuffed with little-used items in the attic.

She had spent her allowance on scented drawer-liner paper from Laura Ashley. It was a lovely, delicate English-looking pattern. Its soft perfume filled the room like a stranger. Jennie would be pleased.

Mom loved matching names. Jodie and Jennie

went together. Of course the twins, Brian and Brendan, went together. Stephen was the oldest, and Mom and Dad had always meant to have a sixth child, who would be named Stacey whether it was a boy or a girl. So there'd have been Jodie and Jennie, Stephen and Stacey, Brian and Brendan.

Of course, after Jennie went missing, nobody could consider another baby. How could any of them ever have left the room again? Nobody could have focused their eyes anywhere else again. They'd all have had heart attacks and died from fear that somebody would take that baby, too.

Jennie was only twenty months younger than Jodie. As toddlers they had fought, Jodie pairing up with Stephen. Over the years, Jodie had thought of this a lot. If she, Jodie, had been holding Jennie's hand at the shopping mall the way she was supposed to, nobody could have kidnapped Jennie.

When she got to know this new sister, should she say she was sorry? Admit that it was her fault? If the new sister said, don't worry, everything's fine now, I'm home and happy, Jodie would be safe telling about her guilt. But if the new sister said, I hate you for it, and I've always hated you for it—what then?

Jodie put the hand mirror that said J E N N I E down on the piece of lace she had chosen to decorate the top of the bureau.

Jodie's mother loved things with names on them. The four kids had mugs, sweatshirts, bracelets, book bags, writing paper—everything—with their names printed or embroidered or engraved. Mom wanted to have a house full of J E N N I E items for the homecoming. It was a popular name. They had had no trouble at the mall finding tons of stuff that said *Jennie.* They bought so much they were embarrassed. "We'll have to bring it out one piece at a time," said Jodie, giggling.

"She'll know we love her," said Jodie's mother.

But behind the hyperventilating and the laughter lay the years of worry.

Mom was trembling. She had been trembling for days. She was actually losing weight from shivering. You could see her hands shake. Nobody had commented on it because everybody else had shivers, too. Everybody was worried about everything. What to serve for dinner on the first night? What to say to the neighbors? How to take Jennie to school. How to hug.

Would she be afraid? Would she be funny? Would she be shy? *What would she be like—this sister who had grown up somewhere else?*

Jodie opened her bureau drawers and looked at the empty halves. She was so proud of herself, opening up her life, just like a drawer, to take Jennie in.

I have a sister again, thought Jodie Spring. She isn't buried. She isn't gone. She wasn't hurt. Her guardian angel did take care of her. And now he's bringing her back to us.

Tomorrow.

2

The bedroom in Connecticut was a beautiful, sunny room, from which Janie Johnson had led a beautiful and sunny life. The leftovers of her childhood enthusiasms filled every shelf: the horseback-riding ribbons from fourth grade; the silver flute and the wooden music stand from sixth; the pompons and trophy from seventh-grade cheerleading.

Janie's mother stared at the room as if she were touring a castle in Europe; as if impossibly distant people had once lived bizarre and unimaginable lives in this room.

But it was their own world that had turned out to be bizarre and unimaginable.

Janie tried to hug her mother, but Mrs. Johnson, the huggingest of people, stepped back. She actually brushed Janie away. "I can't go through any more," whispered her mother. Mrs. Johnson did not look at her daughter, but at the room. The room was all she would have left.

"Don't be mad at me, Mommy," pleaded Janie. How could she go on living if her mother hated her?

Janie felt like a very little girl who needed to sit on her mother's lap.

"I'm not your mother," said Mrs. Johnson in a suspended voice, as if she were being hanged.

Since the truth had come out, Miranda Johnson's elegance had frayed away; she was literally coming apart at the seams. She picked at the pockets and hems of her clothing, unraveling herself.

For Miranda Johnson, motherhood was twice destroyed. Hannah, lost in the remote past, had ruined the present as well.

"You are so my mother!" Janie felt as if her body were going to turn inside out, the way their lives had been turned inside out. Why on earth had she agreed to live with the Springs? Why had she not fought and screamed and refused?

Lawyers had carefully explained that since Janie was not quite fifteen years old—the Johnsons had guessed the baby's age wrong; she was a whole year younger than everybody had thought—she was a minor, and must obey her parents. And her parents were not Mr. and Mrs. Johnson. Her parents were Mr. and Mrs. Spring, who wanted her home. In their house. In their state.

How romantic it had seemed that first week. Real family emerges from shadowy past! Girl discovers bizarre kidnapping, unknown even to the kidnappers!

But it was not romantic. It was the brutal collapse of the woman and man she called Mommy and Daddy.

Janie's friends had long ago stopped calling their parents by baby names. Mother and Dad, or

Mom and Pop, were what other people said. For Janie, her parents were still Mommy and Daddy.

And what had happened to Mommy and Daddy?

Her mother stumbled through their lovely home as if the floor, like life, had come out from under her. Her handsome silver-haired father, who coached school sports during slow seasons in his accounting practice, had become silent and stunned.

It was Janie's fault. She had had choices. She could have said nothing. She could have done nothing. Could have let it go. Let it stay a mystery. She could have chosen to forget the hundred strange things that did not add up.

Janie's head rang with "if only's." If only she had not taken Sarah-Charlotte's milk carton at lunch. She had been given a milk allergy for an important reason: so she would never lay eyes on the photograph of the missing child featured on the milk carton. But one fine autumn day, in the school cafeteria, Janie snitched Sarah-Charlotte's milk.

If only she had tossed that milk carton into the garbage.

If only she had not researched newspaper clippings!

If only she had not told Reeve.

If only Reeve had not told his lawyer sister Lizzie.

And yet . . . the Springs were right. Morally. Weren't they? Wasn't she their child? Didn't she belong with them?

It was too terrifying to think about. Tomorrow

she would get in a car and drive across two state lines and belong to another family. Another family that included three brothers and a sister she had never met. In the midst of overwhelming media attention, she would start classes at a new high school. She could not believe she had to handle so much at once.

How would Mommy and Daddy manage without her?

Downstairs Janie's friends were gathered. It was supposed to be a party. It was a disaster. Sarah-Charlotte had insisted there had to be a good-bye party. It's a big event, Sarah-Charlotte pointed out, which was certainly true. But an event to celebrate? Not at this end, it wasn't.

Janie had no idea, absolutely none at all, how they felt at the other end. The New Jersey end.

She saw New Jersey through a tunnel of fear. She felt as if she were being poured down some evil tube, and she could land in almost anything, and there would be no way out, because she no longer had parents.

Remaining calm was the most important thing. People kept saying to each other, *Now stay calm.* For a while, the Johnsons were all so calm that Reeve wanted to know if they were making night trips to a mortuary and getting embalmed.

Janie's heart softened, thinking of Reeve, who was still funny. But I've lost him, too, she thought. My first boyfriend. My only boyfriend. I can't talk to him either. That's part of the deal. Not talking.

Sunshine filled Janie's bedroom. It was January, and very cold. Ice clung to streets and the branches of trees, but the room was warm and gold.

Janie extended her fingertips. Fearfully, as if choosing to be burned by a hot iron, she touched her mother's shoulder. She broke through. For a moment, touch erased truth.

Mother and daughter hugged, and rocked, and felt each other.

Love, pain, rage, hope, fear—every emotion lost during these last few weeks filled both of them. We weren't calm! Janie thought. We flattened ourselves, so we could fit through this. "Mommy," she whispered, "please don't be mad."

Her mother covered Janie's face with kisses, slowly, as if her lips were memorizing Janie. "I'm not mad at you, honey," said her mother. "How can I be mad at *you*? I love you. You are my life. I'm mad at Hannah! She did this to us. *Twice* she's ruined us."

Hannah. The part of the equation nobody knew, nobody understood, nobody would ever find.

"And most of all, I'm mad at the—" Her mother broke off.

I'm mad at the Springs. That was the sentence. Neither of her parents had said it out loud. Neither had broken down and screamed, *How dare they want you back? You are ours. You are Janie Johnson, not Jennie Spring.*

I'm maddest, Janie realized. I am so mad at the Springs. They kept looking. They put that photograph of their missing daughter on the milk carton. I saw it. And now they're taking me back.

There had not really been any threats. Nobody

15

had said, *Jennie comes to live with us or you go to prison!* It was simply clear, once the facts were known, that this girl was not a Johnson. She was a Spring. She belonged with her birth family.

If Jennie comes back to us, said the Springs through their lawyer, it will not be necessary for us to find Hannah. We will not prosecute her.

For Hannah it must have been a single silly afternoon, probably long forgotten, in which she stole a car and then a kid. But the aftereffects of Hannah's deed rippled on through all their lives. Frank and Miranda Johnson would not survive the criminal trial of their real daughter. They were barely surviving this.

Whoever and whatever Hannah was now, it was imperative that nobody find her.

So Janie had to leave when her parents needed her most, and go to live with strangers. Will they feel like strangers? thought Janie. Will I walk in the door and know that I am home? Will I remember them once we sit down together?

Downstairs the failed party continued.

This was not going away to college, or heading to Europe for the summer. This was not your parents getting terrific promotions and moving to worthy places like California or Texas, so everybody would want to visit you and get letters from you and be envious because you weren't stuck in plain old small-town New England anymore.

This was a party for the end of a person. The name Janie Johnson would vanish into the history of her life. Janie Johnson would drive away, but when she opened that car door in New Jersey, she'd be a girl named Jennie Spring. A girl who had not existed for twelve years.

It was so ironic. In elementary and middle school Janie had detested her name—dull as a phone-book entry. The younger Janie had constantly revised it. Changed Johnson to Jonstone. Changed Janie to Jayyne. Jayyne Jonstone. A name with possibilities, as opposed to the real name, which was lumpy and forgettable.

Well, she had gotten her wish for a different name. And it had more possibilities than any fantasy anyone could have had.

For the mother she was embracing, there might as well be a gravestone with *Janie Johnson* on it.

And that other mother, that biological mother? What was she thinking? That father . . . those new brothers and the sister. Who were they? What was going to happen?

Janie released her mother and walked to the window. She did not know why she had done that—ended the most precious hug of her life. There would not be another one. That intensity, that depth of agony and love—they couldn't bear it again. The next hug, the final good-bye, would be the faked calm they were all so good at now.

There was a knock on the bedroom door. It was not Sarah-Charlotte, because she was downstairs commanding the party. Who else would have the nerve to come upstairs and interrupt Janie and Mrs. Johnson? Janie opened the bedroom door.

Reeve, of course. Who had rescued her from so much, but who could not rescue her from this. She gave him a tight smile. He'll still have my mother, thought Janie. I'll lose Mommy forever, but for Reeve, she'll still be the lady next door. This'll still be the house where he ate half his meals back when his own family was driving him crazy.

Janie was actually jealous. Reeve's parents were really his parents; Reeve's town would still be this town; Reeve's name would still be Reeve.

"People are leaving," said Reeve. He always did that—offering facts, not suggesting an action. Even when Janie confessed that she was the missing child on the milk carton, Reeve had not forced action upon her. He had let her talk, and talk, and talk, when what he wanted was to kiss, and kiss, and kiss.

"Janie!" shouted Sarah-Charlotte up the stairs.

"Coming!" shouted Janie. She marveled at the cheery light in her voice. She took Reeve's hand. She turned her back on the woman standing in the sunny bedroom and went downstairs to rescue the party.

How, thought Janie Johnson, do I go on being happy, when it turns out I enjoyed being kidnapped? How do I face my birth family, when it turns out I cooperated in my own kidnapping? How do the parents I love go on loving me, when I'm the one who turned them in?

CHAPTER
3

Mr. and Mrs. Johnson could not make a long drive on the interstate, fighting traffic, paying tolls, remembering street directions. Not when the journey would end the family.

So one of the lawyers was taking Janie.

Reeve leaned against the dining-room wall, staring out the window, waiting for the lawyer's car to arrive and his mother's permission to go outside and say good-bye. His mother had refused to let him interrupt the Johnsons this morning. Reeve had spent half his life interrupting the Johnsons and was one hundred percent sure of his welcome. He obeyed his mother, but not without a thousand arguments.

Reeve had not slept very well. But he was pretty sure he had slept better than any of the Johnsons.

He loved Janie. Technically she loved him too, but she was divorced from the world right now, and that included Reeve. He had always thought of her as a dizzy redhead, but the word "dizzy" had been a compliment. He thought of Janie as light and airy, like hope and joy. Now "dizzy" meant stumbling and scared, her head swimming with fear.

He thought the promises made by Janie and her parents were wrong, and he thought the Springs were wrong to have asked for them. The promise of silence was terrible. How could Janie not telephone home? Not write? Not visit?

But the Springs wanted their daughter—it was still weird to realize that Janie was somebody else's daughter—to go cold turkey, like giving up cigarettes or booze. Except Janie had to give up her family. As if Mr. and Mrs. Johnson were nothing but an addiction, and three months off would take care of any foolish lingering love.

"It's not as bad as you're making it sound," said Mrs. Shields. She had baked for the occasion. This was how she faced change. She baked for funerals and weddings, she baked for newcomers to the block and friends retiring to Florida. Reeve often wondered about women, but he wondered about his mother most. Why, when Mr. and Mrs. Johnson were saying good-bye to their only child, had his mother made them a chicken, linguini, and olive casserole? Why, when Janie was turning into Jennie, had his mother made her four dozen double-chocolate-chip cookies?

"It is so as bad," said Reeve. His breath had fogged up the window. He rubbed it off with his sweater sleeve.

"If I were the Springs," said his mother, "which thank God I am not, can you imagine wondering where your daughter was for twelve years? I mean, I was crazy when Lizzie disappeared for that one

20

night, do you remember that one terrible night? And Lizzie was eighteen, and still I called the police, but—"

Reeve's mother rarely got to the point. He felt himself losing patience with her, and forced himself to stay motionless. He was supposed to carry the casserole over to the Johnsons, because his mother felt awkward about it. How does she think I feel? thought Reeve.

"—it's really the only way to put something behind you. You have to focus on the new, not the old. So I think it probably is the right way for Janie to make adjustments."

Reeve did not want to be an "adjustment" that Janie had to put behind her. He wanted to be her boyfriend. It was his senior year. He had actually given some thought to senior events, like the prom and graduation dinner.

What were the Springs like? Would they have a sense of humor? Could he call them up and ask if Janie could have a weekend prison pass for the senior prom?

No, he could not call them up. His marching orders, like Janie's, were No Communication.

He thought it would be easier for Janie than for him. She was a little frozen, as if the blizzard of worries had iced her funny laugh and soft skin and adorable smile and—

Oh, well. Reeve blinked away his fantasies of the rest of her. He had not gotten the rest of her; all plans go astray when somebody turns out to be a kidnap victim.

A long, low American four-door, black paint job,

shaded windows, pulled up the Johnsons' driveway. Janie might as well be leaving in a hearse.

I should have made her something, thought Reeve. She doesn't have anything of me to take with her.

When I'm finally allowed to call, will I have to call her Jennie? thought Reeve.

He was suddenly not eager to go outside. He didn't want to go through this either.

"Hold the casserole carefully," instructed his mother. "Tell Janie she'll want to share the cookies with her new family. Now don't drop anything. Latch the door so the wind doesn't get in the house."

Sometimes Reeve couldn't stand women. They were so practical. How could his mother think of drafts and utility bills at a time like this? He turned to tell her for once and for all that he was not going to say good-bye to Janie with a chicken casserole in one hand.

His mother was weeping.

It was like a yawn. He caught it; his own tears fell.

Oh, God, thought Reeve, not a chicken casserole *and* tears.

"Come with me, Mom," he said. He realized as soon as he said it that he needed her. Not to carry her dumb casserole, but to carry some of the horror of this. A mother and father were burying their lives. A girl Reeve loved was driving off into the horizon to God knew what.

Reeve and Mrs. Shields went out of their house and over to the car.

Janie and Mr. and Mrs. Johnson came out at the same moment.

Reeve was so pleased to see that the Johnsons looked good. They must have made a monumental effort for Janie. Mrs. Johnson looked lovely in her scarlet suit, with her gold earrings and chains, her hair nicely curled. Mr. Johnson had shaved for the first time in days, and was in a good pair of cords and a new sweater, with a crisp shirt collar sticking up.

Janie was wearing a heavy coat, hiding her choice of clothing. Janie and Sarah-Charlotte had spent many hours in Janie's closet, discussing what she should wear to greet the Springs. "What do you think, Reeve?" Janie had asked at last.

"Clothes," Reeve had recommended.

Janie looked beautiful. The chaotic mass of red curls was partially tamed by a hairband. One of the things Reeve had to admit he loved about Janie was that he was so big next to her. Reeve had had but one goal through most of his life: to top six feet. Having made that, he yearned for muscles. Having acquired those, he had at last been willing to consider studying. He was not going to get into the best college in the world, but he looked great.

"You look great," whispered Janie.

She had done a lot of whispering lately. He thought: the Springs will be the next people to hear her laugh. He hoped she would be able to laugh. He hoped she would be all right. He hoped she would remember him and not adjust him away.

He hugged her. Very unsatisfying. It was a

neighborly hug, when what Reeve wanted was—well, forget it. He wasn't getting that.

Everybody said good-bye. Everybody was calm. The lawyer shook hands all around. The lawyer opened the passenger door for Janie. Janie looked at the seat as if most people who sat there got electrocuted.

"Mommy?" said Janie.

Her mother seized her, hugging ferociously.

They both kept from crying.

Mrs. Johnson drew a shaky breath and said, one word stumbling slowly after another, "Be our good girl. Make us proud. Show them we were good parents to you."

Just drive away, thought Reeve. This is enough. Get going.

Janie hugged her father one last time. Her father said nothing, just kissed his beloved daughter. A single tear came down his cheek, taking its time, finding every wrinkle and crack.

Janie got in; the lawyer started the engine and reversed out the driveway. If Janie waved, you could not see through the dark glass.

The lawyer shifted into Drive and accelerated down the road. Away to New Jersey.

Mrs. Johnson started to fall.

Her husband and Reeve caught her.

"Don't let Janie see," she whispered.

The black car disappeared. Janie had not seen.

"You'll love this casserole," said Mrs. Shields. "Come on. It's January and we're standing around out here. Let's go in." She shepherded the Johnsons inside their house.

Reeve stood in the driveway a long time. After a while he noticed that he had never given Janie the double-chocolate-chip cookies.

Three months of silence, he thought. It's good I have the cookies. I'm going to need chocolate to last that long.

CHAPTER
4

Stephen was afraid of his own fury.

If he felt like running, he could run off the rage that lived inside him. But he was not an athlete like his younger brothers. Sports annoyed and bored him. Sporadically he went out for a team and found it difficult to get through the season.

Yet his rage settled to the bottom only when he was physically exhausted. Sophomore year he'd made swim team. They had been required to work out in the weight room five mornings a week and swim five afternoons a week. That season, there had been no anger.

But he didn't stay with the swim team. Stephen had never stayed with anything.

Along with the rage was a restlessness.

Stephen disliked being a teenager. He yearned to be gone, to be away from this confining house and these demanding parents.

He never allowed himself to scream at his mother and father. All the self-discipline Stephen had was poured into allowing his parents to live the way they had to live: in fear.

From the day that his sister Jennie disap-peared, when Stephen was only six years old, the Spring household had been ruled by fear.

His mother literally could not live through a child being late. If Stephen said he'd be home at five-fifteen and he got home at five-forty, he would find her white-faced and trembling, pacing the house, hyperventilating, her icy hands touching the telephone and then yanking back. She had a habit of jamming her fingertips fiercely down into the pockets of her jeans. If she ran to the door and her hands were still thrust into her pockets, it meant she was terrified; she was holding on to herself in some desperate way.

She would greet Stephen with the peculiar com-bination of wrath and relief common to all fright-ened parents whose children come home at last.

Except that Jennie had never come home at last.

The family fear extended to many things. Hav-ing lost one child, Stephen's mother and father were terrified of losing another. They fretted about traffic, hot oil in the frying pan, a chain saw, deep water.

They taught their remaining four children to look both ways not only when crossing the street, but also at every other intersection of life: *be cau-tious, be careful, think twice, reconsider, weigh the possibilities.*

Worry was like another person living in the house. A person who, unlike Jennie, never left.

Stephen hated it. He could take care of himself. They lived in New Jersey, and Stephen's daydreams were of the opposite coast: he usually dreamed of

California, occasionally of Oregon, Washington, Utah, Montana, Wyoming. Distant realms, where they could not see him to worry about him. From which he would telephone once a week: *Hi, Mom, I'm fine, life's good, lots of friends, see you at Christmas.*

He had trained his body not to show his fury. He did not clench his fists, he did not grit his teeth, he did not narrow his eyes, he did not turn red or white. The fury instead raced inside his veins, a circulating demon. He had never gone to a counselor, although the family itself often had. He did not want to talk about his wrath, partly because it shamed and mystified him, and partly because it would give his mother and father just one more thing to worry about. They would feel responsible.

But they were not responsible.

Jennie was.

Okay, he knew that was unfair. A little three-year-old who got lost in a shopping center could not be blamed for the following dozen years. He knew this little sister of his, whom he could barely remember, but who had left him a legacy of unending pain and fear, had had suffering of her own.

They should have moved away; they should have left the nightmare of Jennie's kidnapping right in this house, locked the doors and driven away.

The split-level was not large. You came into the house in the middle, of course, on the landing, and went up directly into the kitchen-eating area. To the left was the L-shaped living and dining room. To the right were the bedrooms, two medium and one large, and a single ordinary bathroom. Downstairs

28

were a two-car garage, a laundry room, and a play-room with a fireplace.

When Mr. and Mrs. Spring bought the house, fierce with pride that they had managed to come up with the down payment, they had had two children: Stephen and Jodie. It was the perfect size house. Stephen's bedroom was painted bright barn red and Jodie's bedroom sunshine yellow.

The house quickly became too small: baby Jennie's crib was crowded into Jodie's room and the new twins had to fit into Stephen's. Mr. and Mrs. Spring had their eye on a colonial in another development: a house with four bedrooms and three bathrooms. A house with an immense kitchen, a workshop, and a yard big enough to play football in. They were close to making an offer on the big house on the day that Mrs. Spring took her five children shoe shopping.

Sometimes Stephen still drove down that road, even though it was a dead end and he didn't know anybody who lived there. They never moved. Mr. and Mrs. Spring wanted Jennie to know where to find them.

Even the FBI man, Mr. Mollison, said they could not build the rest of their lives on a missing, and presumably dead, baby girl. Even Mr. Mollison said, as the years went on, "Move. You need the space."

But Mom didn't want a different phone number. She didn't want a different address. "What if . . ." she would begin.

And of course not finish. What possible finish could there be? Jennie was not coming home. Even if she were, a three-year-old wouldn't remember her address or her telephone number. If she had remembered it, she would have phoned them to start with, wouldn't she?

Sometimes, crammed in that tiny bedroom with his twin brothers, Stephen would think: Jennie, it's your fault I don't have a room of my own.

And then of course, would come the slamming guilt, like a door in his face, hitting so hard he should have a bloody nose. Jennie, who had been tortured and left dead in some tangled wood in some other state. Jennie, who had not grown up to have the life she deserved. And he was whining because Brian and Brendan swarmed over him like friendly wasps?

Stephen never felt as if he knew Brian and Brendan. He lived practically on top of them, and yet they remained strangers. They were so enclosed in each other they were like a sealed envelope. Being a twin must be nice, but living with twins was not.

Stephen had plenty of friends. He was popular. But he had never shared his soul the way Brian and Brendan routinely did each other's. The twins did not even have to talk a great deal of the time. They could synchronize without speech.

"I wish," said his mother once, years ago, "that I could synchronize with Jennie like that. That just once, for just one conversation, I could touch Jennie with my mind, my heart, my need."

But Jennie remained hidden in the secret of her disappearance.

Stephen knew kids who believed in ESP—that

with your spirit, if you tried hard enough, you could communicate with another spirit. He knew better. His mother had tried so hard to communicate with Jennie; had listened so carefully to hear Jennie's cries.

But there had been none.

The weird thing was that Stephen's parents were nevertheless very happy people. They adored their four kids. Their lives revolved around family. They were busy and full of laughter. It was just that Jennie was always there.

Or rather, not there.

Her loss lay beneath everything, measuring it.

Sometimes Stephen would see his mother pause at the kitchen sink as she rinsed a dish to go in the dishwasher; see her eyes glaze as she stared out the little window into the backyard. "What are you thinking about, Mom?" he would say, although he knew: she was thinking about Jennie, and whether Jennie was cold, or scared, or hurt.

"Wondering if it's going to rain," his mother would say, turning to smile at him. Her trembling smile, her cover-up smile.

Sometimes Stephen would go along with her. "I don't think it's that cloudy," he'd say.

Sometimes Stephen had to open the wound. "She's dead, Mom. And that means she's okay. She's not cold or scared or hurt."

Sometimes, when he was older, and especially after he became taller than his mother, he would put his arms around her and silently hold her, and feel her pain right through the fold of his embrace.

* * *

31

One week before Christmas, Stephen was nuking himself a hot dog. The twins had a basketball game at six-thirty and nobody had time for a real supper. Jodie was eating ravioli straight from the can, an act so disgusting that Stephen had to turn his back. "You look like a possum eating from the garbage pail."

Dad, holding his own hot dog into his mouth while chewing at the tip, ran to the bedroom to yank off his suit and get into his favorite cords and his bright red, team-color sweater. Mom had toasted bagels for herself and was spreading cream cheese, muttering about whether she would have time to brush her teeth before they had to pile in the car and head for the middle school. Brendan and Brian were both starters, so it was important to arrive for the first minute of play.

In the living room behind them, the star on the Christmas tree scraped the ceiling. Presents were stacked five deep under the lowest branches. Stephen had outgrown the need to squeeze and pinch but the twins had been ducking under the tree for days, feeling up the gifts. A silver bowl filled with glittering glass Christmas balls sat in the middle of the dining table, but like all the Springs' decorating choices, it was largely hidden by mail, homework, receipts, and unread newspapers. The refrigerator was completely covered with Christmas cards, which they would open and reread while on the phone.

Stephen bit off half the hot dog and concentrated on not choking to death.

The phone rang. He would have answered, but

his mouth was pretty full, so Mom shifted her bagel to the other hand, grabbed the phone off the wall, and said, "Hello?"

They were a fair-complexioned family, redheads with translucent skin that tanned poorly. But they were not actually white, of course, like sheets of paper. Mom turned white. The color left her face so dramatically that Stephen actually looked at the floor to see if blood had puddled at her feet. Her eyes opened extremely wide, then fluttered closed. He got up to catch her, thinking that she was fainting, that something terrible must have happened. Somebody had died—somebody—

"It's Jennie," whispered his mother. "She saw her picture on the milk carton."

A month ago.

A month filled with his parents' hope and his own anger. Resentment that Stephen could taste backwashed in his mouth. It ruined every meal.

I'm going to adjust, he told himself. I'm the oldest. I have to set an example.

All he could think of was cramming yet another person into this tiny house.

CHAPTER
5

The first few days were such a blur, Janie wondered if she needed glasses. Or a tranquilizer. Maybe a guidebook. Maybe a guide dog.

She was physically afraid.

It was absurd. For the first time in twelve years, she was with her real family, in her real house. And for the first time in twelve years, she was truly frightened. She was not the bright, sophisticated daughter of Frank and Miranda Johnson; she had weirdly, terrifyingly, turned into the three-year-old daughter of Jonathan and Donna Spring. Her vocabulary fell away; she could speak only in monosyllables. Her view of the world was so limited she might have been three feet tall, while the strangers around her were towering monsters.

They are not monsters, she told herself. They are your real parents. Your real brothers. Your real sister. You started this. Now you have to leap in. Come on in, Janie, the water's fine.

But she hovered on the edge of the pool, so to speak, unable to dip a toe into the water, let alone start swimming.

It was so strange to be sitting among people who looked like her. Thick masses of red curly hair went all the way around the table.

Her new sister Jodie's red hair was very short, a circle of fine silky curls that she never brushed. Jodie was pretty, in a pixieish way. She was also very noisy in sleep. Jodie turned and thrashed and moaned. She flung the covers off during the night. She went to sleep with a rock station on and left the radio playing.

Except for spending the night at Sarah-Charlotte's, or Adair's, which were special occasions and hardly ever involved sleep, Janie had never shared a bedroom. It turned out that sharing a bedroom with Jodie Spring hardly ever involved sleep either. And even if she could get used to Jodie's breathing and thrashing, every sound in the house was wrong and threatening.

Her new twin brothers, Brian and Brendan, the sixth-graders, had hair so red and gold it glittered. She could not tell them apart. They were not identical; it was the names that did her in. If one had had a B name and the other something completely different, she would have done better. But she kept calling Brian Brendan and Brendan Brian. They did not like it. She did not blame them.

"You want we should wear name tags?" said Brendan at last. Or else Brian.

Janie swallowed and tried to keep smiling. "Maybe a clue. What's my guideline?"

"I'm handsomer," said Brendan. "I have more freckles, browner eyes, and more girlfriends." He grinned. He also had teeth more in need of braces.

35

Brendan—braces, thought Janie. Remember that. Now as long as he keeps his mouth open, you'll know who he is.

Her oldest brother was Stephen. His hair was a darker red, and lay smoothly. He combed it frequently. Stephen was tall and skinny, with immense feet. It was difficult to believe that a human being could have feet that large. You had to assume that his body would grow to match, in which case Stephen would become a man of splendid proportions.

Stephen's eyes settled on Janie with a sort of vengeful dislike. Perhaps he wished that Janie had just been killed back when she was three. It would have been so much easier, emotionally, to have found a grave marker instead of a living stranger.

Even being afraid of Stephen, Janie found it easier to look at him, or at Jodie, or Brendan, or Brian, than to look at her new parents. She felt no connection whatsoever with this man and woman. She might as well have gone into some bank or grocery and been told to call the managers Mom and Dad.

She could not hug them. The imprint of her mother's last hug clung to her like a beloved perfume. The brush of her father's last kiss was still on her forehead.

So she called them Mr. and Mrs. Spring. It was ridiculous, and yet what else was she supposed to do?

Mostly she managed not to call anybody anything. She pasted on a quivering facsimile of a smile, her lips as dead as if the dentist had given her Novocain.

They called her Jennie, of course. That's who she was. The girl they had spent twelve long years searching for. It made Janie feel as if she had an invisible twin; as if, like Brendan, she had a Brian close by. When they said "Jennie" it never felt that they were talking to her, Janie.

Get a grip, Janie told herself over and over.

She tried breathing deeply, she tried meditating, she tried lecturing herself, she even tried praying, which she had never come across before. Her family was not religious. But the Springs were. They prayed every night before supper, a lengthy grace, during which they held hands.

Who were these people? They could not be her family.

Mrs. Spring was very talkative. Stories about her day poured out of her. She laughed, teased, and interrogated her kids about every quiz, ball game, and book report. She was revved up at high speed, whipping through her own workday, charging into her kids' afterschool activities. She was always out of breath and halfway into her next move.

Mr. Spring was very physical with his kids. He picked them up as if they were still toddlers. He wrestled with the boys, he bear-hugged, he threw pillows at them, he raced them to see who would get the TV remote control. Janie shrank back, keeping herself near a wall or large furniture, lest he hoist her into the air, too.

The house even smelled different. The scrubbed quiet of the Johnson home was such a contrast to this house full of boys' sneakers and athletic jackets thrown on the floor while baseballs, bats, and mitts were left for anybody to trip over in the hallways.

Nothing was right. Even breakfast was wrong. The Springs had apple juice, not orange juice. Anybody knew you had to start the day with orange juice. They had instant oatmeal, the flavored kind in individual envelopes. It tasted like cedar chips for hamsters. She wanted cinnamon toast and half a grapefruit. They didn't even have bread in their house! Nobody ate sandwiches. How could you get through life without sandwiches?

Homesickness actually made her sick. Her stomach hurt. Once with Reeve, who had in mind driving around to find a dark secluded spot to be alone with his girl, Janie had gotten so sick from what she was starting to understand that she made Reeve pull over so she could throw up in the bushes. She felt that way all the time here.

I'll never be able to swallow again, she thought, so what difference does it make if they don't have sandwiches?

There was only one bathroom.

Janie had had her own bath all her life.

She could not believe she had to share a bathroom with six other people! They had a timer you had to set before you took a shower. You could use hot water for exactly three minutes, then you had to get out. Three minutes! Janie couldn't even get wet that fast.

Nor was there room in the bathroom to keep anything but your toothbrush in there. Everybody had a plastic pail in which to carry their shampoo and shower cap and stuff back and forth.

People were always lined up for the bathroom. And if Janie got in, they grilled her. "What are you going to do in there?" they demanded. "Hurry up. I have to do my makeup." "I have to leave in five minutes." "You wait for me instead, Jennie."

This family did not know what leisure was.

They were stacked up like planes for landing.

When they were not studying her, or in line ahead of her, or serving her food that was completely different from the food she had grown up on, they were asking her trick questions.

"Would you like to look at your baby pictures?" said Mrs. Spring.

On the one hand, Janie would love to see her baby pictures. On the other hand, that was one of the things that had forced Janie's back against the wall in Connecticut: her parents had no photographs of Janie as a little girl. After a pause in which Janie weighed the possibility of looking at these baby pictures, and seeing herself among these people as a family, in their arms, in their high chair, in their car seat, she pressed her lips together and shook her head no.

"It isn't being disloyal to Mr. and Mrs. Johnson to start liking us, Jennie," said Mrs. Spring softly.

Janie began to cry.

"I know you're not ready to call me Mom, or call your father Dad," said Mrs. Spring, beginning to cry herself. "I know those are precious syllables. I know this is going to take time, and it's going to hurt. But it's okay to relax here, Jennie. It's okay to have a good time, or laugh, or even let somebody hug you."

I'm not *Jennie!* she thought. I'm *Janie!* She managed a nod. She managed to let Mrs. Spring put both arms around her. She stood very still inside the hug and could not imagine that she would ever hug back. But she was able to receive one.

"Whew!" teased Brendan. Or Brian. "Wipe the sweat off your brow, Jennie. You survived a hug! Give that girl a medal!"

She did have to laugh.

"Pretend it's overnight camp," said Jodie. Jodie had the same large brown eyes as the twins. She tossed her head in the same teasing stance as her mother. "So you're a little homesick the first week. Pretty soon it's the best time you've ever had."

The best time she had ever had? Janie choked. She had been there only one weekend, and it felt like a hundred abandoned years. Her thoughts were so chaotic they did not even feel like thoughts, but a jumble of nightmare that meant nothing and went nowhere.

This time it was Mr. Spring who tried to hug her. He was so big and his red beard so foreign and intrusive. She backed away from him as if he were a grizzly bear. Behind the curling mustache, his face collapsed. She had hurt him. Stephen and Jodie exchanged looks that Janie could not read. Only the twins seemed disinterested. As for Mrs. Spring— Janie could not look at her. How could your mother —the most important person in your childhood— turn out to be somebody else? She could never, never, never use the word "mother" on Mrs. Spring.

Be our good girl. Make us proud. Show them we were good parents to you.

"I'm sorry," Janie said. "I'm trying. I really am. But it's—it's hard. I've been taken away from my real family *twice*." She didn't want to cry. She didn't want them to see how scared she was.

"Except the Johnsons weren't your real family," said Mr. Spring carefully. "They were wonderful people, and we will always be in debt to them, because they took care of our daughter for us. But you're *back* with your real family, sweetie."

She didn't want strangers calling her sweetie.

"Anyway," said Jodie, getting mad, "we didn't take you from the Johnsons. *You* called *us*. You're the one who recognized yourself on the milk carton. You wanted to come here."

"I *didn't* want to come," Janie mumbled. "I just wanted you to know that I was all right. I wanted you to stop worrying." Now it was her parents in Connecticut doing the worrying. They too had lost a daughter twice. *Oh, Mommy!* she thought, her lungs flaring up like bonfires. I can't even breathe here, Mommy. I want to go home!

"We love you, Jennie," said Mrs. Spring. She ran her fingers through Janie's hair as if she owned Janie. As if she were Janie's mother. "And we're very, very glad to have you home."

6

"The first day of school," said Mrs. Spring, "will probably be difficult for you, Jennie. There's been a lot of publicity."

Janie had always loved Mondays, because she had always loved school. School was where your friends waited for you, where your boyfriend waved to you, and where your teachers thought you were terrific.

A new family on Friday and a new school on Monday. It was too much!

What is it like to be a foster child? thought Janie. And have new families all the time?

She could not find a safe place to look. There were so many staring eyes in this big family. She refused to let herself start at a new school with tears running down her cheeks. She hung on to her thoughts and was painfully grateful to be handed a notebook to hold also. J E N N I E, it said in big white letters embossed on the slick blue front.

These people were in love with their own names. So far they had given her not only a mug emblazoned J E N N I E, but also a juice glass, a spoon, and a dozen pencils. Even her pale blue pillowcase was embroidered in lacy, loopy white script, J E N N I E.

I'm Janie. Janie, Janie, Janie.

She held the notebook upside down so she would not have to look at the lettering. She forced herself to look at Mrs. Spring. Chunky and going gray, Mrs. Spring was not interested in clothing. She had yanked on a skirt and blouse that didn't quite match and a sweater that didn't quite hang right. She wore a utility watch with a plain black strap.

Janie and her mother both had Swatch collections, and liked to choose a watch for the day that matched earrings and other accessories.

Jodie had helped pick out clothes for the first day of school that would be just like what the rest of the New Jersey kids wore. She was amazed at the size of Janie's wardrobe. "There's nothing you don't have," Jodie said, fingering the thirty Swatches and the growing tower of sweaters. Jodie had graciously cleared drawers and hangers, but the space did not hold a fraction of Janie's possessions. The girls looked at each other uneasily and Janie was embarrassed by the collection that only a few weeks ago she had thought was skimpy and needed replenishing. "I guess we'll just shove the rest of this under the beds or something."

"They're rich, aren't they?" said Jodie.

Jodie meant her parents. Should Janie say—Yes, my parents are rich—in which case she would be told—They aren't your parents? Should she say—Well, not rich in comparison to Reeve's family;

43

Reeve's family is really rich. Then she'd have to explain Reeve.

Reeve.

There would be no boy next door to give her rides to school. No boy to swagger down the hall with his arm around her, boasting with his walk that he dated this girl. There would be no grin across the cafeteria, no snack sharing at Janie's after school, no phone call at night.

Three months before I can talk to Reeve again, thought Janie. I can't believe we agreed to three months of silence!

She forgot to answer Jodie's question about the Johnsons' money.

"Time to go," said Jodie in a funny voice.

Janie took a quick look in the long mirror fastened to the back of Jodie's bedroom door. First-day-of-school horrors hit the pit of her stomach. She could never tell, on the first day of school, whether she was attractive and likable, or geeky and pathetic, doomed to be ignored and taunted.

"You look great," said Jodie eagerly. "You look just like a Spring."

Janie did not want to look like a Spring. She wanted to look like a Johnson. Reflected in the truth of the mirror, with Jodie's pixie face behind her, Janie knew once and for all there had been no error. She was a Spring.

"I'll stay with you as long as I can," said Jodie, "but you're in a different grade. You'll have different classes. But each teacher has assigned you a buddy. You won't ever have to go anywhere alone."

Janie nodded.

Mrs. Spring drove them, so Janie didn't have to face the bus yet. When the girls got out of the car, she said, like a mother, "Be brave, honey. It'll be a long day, but each day will be easier." Jodie gave her mother a good-bye kiss, but Janie got out of the car quickly and faced the next torture.

It was a generic high school. Vanilla-painted cement block. Black-and-gray-speckled vinyl floors. Fluorescent strip lighting. Art projects trying to lighten the place up.

She tried to blend in. She tried to be anonymous, the way new kids were supposed to be. But they knew her. It was equal parts romantic and hideous. The other students were fascinated and yet repelled, as if her kidnapped state might be infectious. I don't have to worry about being ignored, she thought ruefully.

A sort of home video played in Janie's mind. She saw not the new faces around her, but the old ones she should have been with on a Monday. Her real parents, friends, teachers, and neighbors surrounded her in a cloud of loss.

Miranda Johnson would be getting ready for her day at the hospital. Although volunteers wore repulsive salmon-pink jackets, Janie's mother nevertheless dressed beautifully. She had an entire wardrobe that would look terrific with that ugly half-red. Janie imagined her mother, going through her silent routines, in her silent house, heading for the hospital.

But what if her mother could not pick up the routines? What if she just sat home, frozen in an empty house? *Oh Mommy! Please be all right!*

General Chorus was on Janie's new schedule. They'd been able to duplicate all her Connecticut subjects except one: silversmithing. Janie was not artistic and had never succeeded at any craft from cross-stitch to cake decorating, but she had always wanted to make her own jewelry.

General Chorus instead. Wonderful.

Janie could not sing. She had roughly a four-note range, considerably lower than female voices ought to be. The choir director back home used to yell at the altos, "Somebody get out of the basement!" The somebody was Janie, and she could not get her voice out of the basement. Although she loved music and wished passionately for a voice, she had dropped chorus years ago.

Knowing what her voice would do to the harmony, Janie did not even attempt to sing. It was nice to have a black music folder though. It was nice to be in a room of eighty kids whose attention was on somebody else—the conductor.

Miss P was very funny. She picked on everybody, all the time, but it was not cruel and nobody's feelings were hurt. Even Janie, who knew nobody and shared no in-jokes, found herself laughing. It was such a treat to laugh out loud. At her Connecticut school, boys rarely joined the choir, because they were so afraid of becoming Chorus Geeks. This had a different atmosphere: the best boys were here —jocks, studs, and scholars. All of them in love with Miss P.

Miss P dragged a very nervous young man to the front of the room. He wore a suit, but it looked like somebody else's, or as if somebody else had dressed him for the day. Janie knew the feeling.

"Hey, guys!" shouted Miss P.

"Miss P!" they shouted back.

"I brought you a new victim," said Miss P. "A student teacher."

"All right!" shouted the boys. "Fair game!"

The young man struggled to look brave and competent. He lost.

"Mr. Clarke," said Miss P, swinging her arms in the direction of the chorus, "welcome to the land that normalcy forgot."

The bass section sprang into wrestling poses, proud of living in the land that normalcy forgot.

Janie could breathe a little better. The boys in the bass section reminded her of Reeve. You could fall in love with one of them. She smiled at Miss P. She smiled at Mr. Clarke, who was so afraid he could hardly lift his arms to direct. I can't lift my arms to hug, she thought. I've got to learn in public, too. Good luck, Mr. Clarke!

Janie's seatmate was an alto named Chrissy, who had been assigned to her. Chrissy was long and lean and reminded Janie of Reeve's annoying older sister Lizzie. Even though Janie had detested Lizzie all her life, she found herself homesick for her.

"You need to check yourself off on the attendance sheet," said Chrissy softly. She pointed toward four large oaktag posters—Soprano, Alto, Tenor, Bass—one name to a line.

"I'm not on it," Janie whispered back. "I looked when I came in."

Chrissy looked at her oddly. "Yes, you are. We

47

redid the entire alto section to put you in. Miss P said you were going to feel weird enough and she wanted your name in alphabetical order."

After chorus Chrissy dragged her right up to the alto poster. "See?" she said, pointing.

Spring, it said. *Jennie.*

I was looking under J for Johnson, thought Janie. I never thought of looking under S for Spring.

Eighty General Chorus members drifted past, slowing the usual rampage to get to the next class, fascinated by the presence of the kidnap victim and pretending not to be. Janie could feel Miss P's eyes on her, and a question forming on Mr. Clarke's lips.

"They had an assembly about you," said Chrissy.

Janie froze.

"The whole school," said Chrissy. "All seven hundred of us. The principal told us the whole story so there would be no questions. He said you were going through a lot and we were not to poke into things that weren't our business, or make trouble. He said every adolescent asks who he is, and why he drew the parents he did, but you must be asking yourself more than any teenager in America."

Janie could have thrown up on Chrissy. The whole school had attended an assembly to discuss Janie Johnson's personal problems? The invasion of it! The trespass!

"Did my—um—" she could not quite say the nouns out loud. She took a shuddery breath and started up again. "Did my brother and sister go?" There. She had called Stephen and Jodie her brother and sister. Out loud. Wipe the sweat off my brow, she thought, remembering Brian. Or Brendan.

"Of course they went. Everybody went."

"Did they talk?"

"No. They're very closemouthed about the whole thing." Chrissy waited, wide-eyed and hopeful. She wanted Janie to talk. She wanted gossip and detail.

I want gossip and detail, too, thought Janie. I want to talk so much I can hardly bear it. I want to be on the phone with Sarah-Charlotte. I want to be in the backseat with Reeve. I want—

Janie was afraid she was going to bawl right in the chorus room. She moved quickly on, before Miss P could get any closer. Music teachers were always understanding. Janie was not ready.

"Give me your schedule," ordered Chrissy. She took it out of Janie's hands before Janie could react. "Okay. You go to English next. Mrs. Fann. I liked Mrs. Fann, but your sister hated her! They fought all last year. Your parents were in here all the time, arguing about Mrs. Fann's assignments and standards and grading."

It was so surprising, somehow, that the Springs had been having a life when Janie had not even known they existed. Parents arguing and sisters fighting. She was dizzy with understanding that this family was *real*. "All last year" meant the last school year. Before the milk carton. Before Reeve. Back when Janie Johnson had truly been a little girl, knowing nothing, wondering about nothing.

The good old days, thought Janie. "Thanks, Chrissy," she said, when Chrissy turned her over to Mrs. Fann.

I have to be polite, she thought. I'm going to live here. With the Springs. I'm going to graduate from high school here. With Chrissy. With Miss P. With Mrs. Fann.

I'm not going to move home, or get transferred, or leave for college.

This is it.

"So what's she like?" demanded Nicole.

Jodie shrugged.

"She's so pretty!" said Caitlin. "I love her hair. It's like yours, only about a yard more of it."

Yes, Jennie was Dad's daughter all right. All the way down the long school corridors, Jodie could see the resemblance. Jennie had a wild, chaotic mane of red curls, just like Dad's, except in Dad it was the beard that crinkled and curled. They stood alike and lifted their chins alike. Jodie could not get over it. It made her heart turn over.

Jennie must have been as distinctive when she was three, the angry middle child who never felt she got enough attention—who was happy to let a strange woman buy her a sundae and take her for a joyride.

"So?" pressed Caitlin. "Tell us about her."

Jodie had thought talking about the new sister would be the most fun thing. But it wasn't. Jennie was no wonderful roommate. She was a stranger who wanted to be called by her kidnapped name, Janie, and who didn't want to cooperate in anything. She'd been back exactly three days and Jodie was already completely exhausted living with her.

Jennie didn't eat what was set in front of her.

50

She didn't meet their eyes, or laugh, or tell stories. She was just there. Trembling.

Nicole leaned closer to Jodie and lowered her voice, as if they were telling secrets. Nicole and Caitlin were thrilled to be best friends with the girl whose kidnapped sister had been returned home. They were hoping for some really gory details. So far nobody had any details, even boring ones. "Have you talked about any of the good stuff yet? Like what really happened?"

Jodie shook her head. Her throat closed up.

The thing is, thought Jodie, that my feelings are hurt. I love my family. I think we are absolutely terrific. I have this handsome, bear-hug Dad with a beard and a head full of jokes who's crazy about us, and always wants everybody on a sports team so he can cheer and stomp his feet and take videos that nobody ever looks at afterwards. I have this exhausted mother going gray who works too hard but loves it, because she's so crazy about her kids and her husband. She sells hot dogs and soda at halftime at the twins' games because she and Dad chair the Athletic Boosters. She never lets anybody miss Mass. She loves buying me clothes, because I'm the only girl. No matter how tired she is after work, she makes a real dinner, because she loves it when we hold hands and say grace, and it's hard to say much in the way of grace over a pizza delivered to the door.

I love our town. I love our school. I love my friends.

Jodie had been excited about showing off all those things. She had expected the new sister to be thrilled with the Springs. Awestruck that she belonged to such neat people. She had expected Jennie to clap her hands, maybe. Burst into song. Instead Jennie kept her back to the wall and her elbows sticking out to fend off hugs.

Not only that, Jodie was battling jealousy. This girl had everything. There was not one watch, one scarf, one jacket, one necklace that the Johnsons had not given her. It was as if a department store had moved into Jodie's bedroom.

Caitlin said, "It's bad?"

Jodie shrugged. "Jennie gets into bed at night as if it's a hiding place."

"Gulp," said Nicole. "What are you guys doing to her?"

"We're not doing anything to her! We're trying really hard. She's the one who's not trying." Jodie could not bear it that her sister dream was not coming true. And even more she could not bear it that the parent dream was not coming true for Mom and Dad. Jennie wouldn't let them near her.

"Jennie's the one who's scared," Nicole pointed out. "I'd be scared too if I had lost my mother and father."

"Jennie did not lose her parents," said Jodie fiercely. "She got them back."

Nicole shrugged eyebrows, shoulders, and hands all at the same time. "Maybe she only wants the other set."

Caitlin swatted Nicole with a math workbook. "Try a little tact, will you?" She tried to console Jodie. "It'll take time, that's all, Jo," she said.

"Time!" said Jodie, furious. The temper on

which she had so little grip erupted. "We've spent twelve years missing Jennie! Now we're supposed to spend—what—another twelve years helping her work back into the family?"

"Now come on," said Caitlin. "This is just day four, right?"

Jodie nodded.

"I bet it takes twelve months," said Nicole. "Yup. How much money do you want to bet that it's a whole year before Janie turns into Jennie?"

A year? How could they stand it?

"When is the FBI coming over?" asked Nicole.

Jodie was starting to find Nicole very tiresome. "Next week, supposedly. Or maybe never. My parents won't let them talk to her until she's settled in. At the rate Jennie's settling in, Hannah will have died of old age before we get the facts."

"I can't wait to hear more about Hannah," said Nicole. She actually rubbed her palms together with anticipation.

Jodie had almost forgotten the kidnapper, in the reality of dealing with the kidnapped. They had never seen a picture of Hannah, this woman who had ripped Jennie Spring off a soda-fountain stool in a mall and carried her away. Hannah, who had brutalized their family with one short car drive.

Newcomers to Highview Avenue were always astonished by the way the Spring family worked. The kids did not have baby-sitters, on the theory that a sitter would not know how to deal with a kidnapper. Either Uncle Paul and Aunt Luellen baby-sat, or else Mom and Dad did not leave. Even now, with Stephen seventeen and Jodie sixteen, Mom notified the neighbors if she was going to be out of reach for so much as an hour. Old friends would explain in a whisper: "They lost a child, you know. Kidnapped. They're very paranoid."

They weren't paranoid, though. That meant overly suspicious. People whose little girl had been kidnapped could never be too suspicious.

Oh, Hannah! What you did to us!

"Yes," said Jodie, hating Hannah. "I want some details, too."

CHAPTER

7

The Spring family did not "do" things the way her real family did. Nobody visited museums. Nobody went to antique shows. Nobody got theater tickets. Nobody belonged to the symphony series. Nobody sat quietly at the dining-room table reading the newspaper. In fact, nobody sat quietly.

Instead, the house filled with Spring children and Spring friends.

On her second Saturday, a horde of the twins' friends materialized at the house. Janie expected Mrs. Spring to go insane from the noise and the mess, but she just laughed and pushed the boys downstairs into the family room. They popped up constantly, demanding food or drink, throwing Nerf balls at everybody, and screaming at the rain outside to turn into enough snow to cancel school on Monday.

Stephen's friends Mark and Drew—boys she could have had a crush on if her mind had been free —came over to play SuperNintendo with Stephen. The three of them sat on the floor in front of the living-room television, which had the game hookup.

The short, burbly song of each game repeated end-lessly. Stephen, Mark, and Drew played all day long, falling backward on the floor, screaming, "I'm dead, I'm dead!" when they got killed.

The twins' crowd was mostly having cookies: Oreos, chocolate chip, and lemon wafers. Stephen's trio was having nachos, and were continually in the kitchen shredding cheese and lettuce, chopping to-matoes and olives, and loading plates into the mi-crowave.

Jodie's friend Nicole came over. Nicole had en-tered a fashion contest with a five-hundred-dollar prize for Most Unlikely Material for a Dress. Nicole had struggled to make a dress out of her little brother's millions of Legos but it didn't work and now she had a minidress of her mother's from the sixties and was tediously sewing Matchbox cars all over it. Janie had never seen anything so pathetic in her life.

Through all this, Mr. Spring came and went from the attached garage where he was changing the oil or something in the cars. Mrs. Spring was on the phone at the same time that she was leafing through women's magazines, doing a crossword, and updating her address book from a tower of Christmas cards she was getting ready to throw out.

The black-and-white kitchen TV, tuned to CNN, droned stories of politics, earthquakes, and federal funding for art projects.

The noise and the chaos were incredible.

Janie sat at the kitchen table, untouched homework spread in front of her. She had wedged herself safely into a corner, where she could hear and see everything but was not in the direct line of traffic. It was probably just as well she could not telephone Sarah-Charlotte to describe this place. It was not only a zoo; now that Nicole had arrived, Janie was the chief exhibit.

Nicole was dying to hear about the kidnapping. "Have you been to the mall yet, Jennie?" she said. "You know. The one where—well—you know."

Janie shook her head and pretended to write in her science-lab notebook.

"Here, Jennie," said Nicole. "I've threaded a needle for you. Start sewing this row of cars onto the dress. There's room at the table for all three of us to work on it. I'll never get it done without you."

Janie had never held a sewing needle in her life.

She could possibly imagine sewing a torn hem. But she could not believe that her first sewing project involved tacking a two-inch car onto a mini-dress.

It was remarkably hard. You had to wind the thread around the tiny axles of the car, or through the little windows. The car had to be attached in at least two places to keep it from sagging. Janie concentrated. When she had sewn on a royal-blue car, she sorted through the rest of the cars and picked out a miniature ambulance to go next to it. Then she added a red convertible.

"Try it on," commanded Jodie, thrusting the dress back into Nicole's arms.

Nicole had already tried it on three times. But she obligingly tugged it on again. What had seemed pitifully ridiculous when there were just a couple of cars sewn on was now so weird that it was fabulous.

"I like it!" said Janie, laughing. "It's going to be like armor. You're a medieval knight, except on the interstate."

"Was the interstate built when you were kidnapped?" said Nicole. "Did that woman drive you away on I-95?"

Mrs. Spring, despite phone, crosswords, Nintendo songs, CNN, and address book, was paying attention. "Nicole," she said sharply.

"I'm just asking."

"Just wear your dress, Nicole. If you feel the need to ask another question, fill your mouth with a cookie."

Suddenly, like the next act of a play, or perhaps a different play altogether, the scene changed. Mr. Spring kicked Stephen, Mark, and Drew out of the living room so he could watch sports on television; a parent arrived in a van and siphoned off all the twins' friends; Mrs. Spring got off the phone and began preparing spaghetti sauce. This consisted of browning some hamburger and sausage and onions and throwing in two immense jars of store-bought sauce and then adding—over the twins' moans and protests—a big freezer box of broccoli.

"Stir this," she said to Janie, and Janie stood up right where she was sewing, reached across the small kitchen and stirred slowly with the wooden spoon.

I wonder if I'll ever get used to this, she thought. The way they live. The noise they make.

And Janie Johnson realized, with a sick lurch, that she was used to it. She was enjoying herself. The family was still something to watch rather than take part in, but these people were no longer aliens from outer space; they were nice and bumped into each other and cooked spaghetti by the vat.

She couldn't start liking them! How would her mother feel if Janie had a good time?

The twins came into the kitchen to sample the sauce, letting no vegetable contaminate their spoonfuls.

"You should have covered your dress with plastic horses, Nicole," said Brendan. "Remember how you used to own twelve thousand My Pretty Ponies?"

"Six," said Nicole. "I had six of them."

Everybody laughed. Mrs. Spring went down the hall. Mr. Spring turned up the volume on the TV so he could hear over the kitchen laughter.

"I used to ride," said Janie, feeling that she was acting dangerously by participating at all; this was like bungee-jumping, to join the Springs in conversation.

"Real horses?" said Jodie, amazed and impressed.

Janie nodded. "I took lessons for three years. I entered lots of shows. The way the stables do it, so that everybody triumphs, they make sure you're in a riding class with very few others. That way you're bound to get a ribbon. I got tons of ribbons but I was never much of a rider. The third horse I owned was hard to manage and I lost interest."

She had said something wrong. They were staring at her.

"I thought you said you took gymnastics and flute," said Stephen.

He was angry. Janie could not imagine what made him angry. "All the girls took flute. Sixth grade," said Janie. "Every girl I knew started flute and every boy started drums or trumpet."

"How did your parents afford all those lessons?" said Brendan.

"Her parents were rich," said Brian.

"They were not her parents," said Stephen. "Stop calling them that."

"They were my parents," said Janie. "I didn't have any others."

"Here!" said Stephen, stabbing the kitchen-table top with his index finger. "You had parents *here*."

"I didn't know anybody was here," said Janie.

"Of course you did!" Stephen's anger spilled over. "You had to have known! You had to have said to these wonderful perfect rich terrific Johnsons— Oh, by the way, my name is actually Jennie Spring, mind taking me home?"

He had touched on the evil in the story. He was right. Why hadn't she argued? Why hadn't she told them her real name? And if she had, *why hadn't the Johnsons listened?* "I don't remember. It's a long long time ago. I don't know what I said to anybody."

She wished Mr. or Mrs. Spring would come into the room. She wished Nicole were not there, with her eyes hot for gossip.

"You were three," said Stephen. "That's old enough for complete sentences. That's old enough for arguing. That's old enough to make it clear who you are."

"I know that," said Janie. "Do you think I

60

haven't wondered why I didn't fight Hannah? I didn't scream, or try to break free, or anything. I just went along for the ride and had a good time. Do you think it isn't awful to live with that?"

Brendan, trying for once in his dumb life to be a peacemaker, spoke up. "It wasn't your fault, Jennie," said Brendan. "It was those terrible people. Those horrible Johnsons. You probably told them over and over that they had no right to keep you. They must have lied to you millions of times until eventually you believed them. They probably tortured you. You probably have scars. You've just blocked all that out."

Janie leapt up from the table. Matchbox cars spewed over the floor. Jodie's glass of Coke tipped onto Nicole's fashion entry.

"Shut up!" screamed Janie. "They are not terrible people! They didn't know what was happening! If they had known, they wouldn't have let it. They are wonderful people. I love them. And they *are* my parents. So there!"

CHAPTER
8

The shape of the room in which she had English was different from the classroom in Connecticut. The slant of the sunlight coming through the windows was different. The test, however, was just an English test. One page with thirty easy short-answer questions.

Janie had done her homework last night. In fact, she had done her homework more thoroughly than at any time in her life. Otherwise she would have had to join in.

But at the top of the upper right hand corner of the one-page test was something Janie had not bargained for.

*Name:*_____

It was her eleventh day in New Jersey, and her sixth day in school. She had not had to pass in homework before, and she had not had to take an exam until today.

No one else on earth, thought Janie, is taking this particular test. No one else on earth has to pass. No one else on earth has two possible answers to that question. *Name:*_____

The Springs might claim that Janie Johnson and Jennie Spring were the same. Janie knew better. They were two entirely separate human beings, and their lives and experiences had not overlapped in twelve years.

Janie held that pencil very tightly. She wrote a single letter. J.

I'm J no matter what, she thought. That's all I have left for sure. One capital letter.

She closed her eyes. The yellow angles of the pencil pressed against the soft pads of her fingers. She opened her eyes and swiftly scribbled the thirty answers, finishing before anybody else. Briefly she looked up. Mrs. Fann was studying her with intense fascination.

All eyes looked over and around and through Janie now, as if she were public property, as if they deserved the rest of the answers.

There was only one answer. Janie and the family she loved had agreed on the answer. There were a lot of reasons, but the biggest was to protect Mommy and Daddy from having to go through anything more. From having to think any more about what Hannah did. She could no longer be Janie Johnson. Today she had to admit it. Forming each letter carefully, using her best script.

Name: Jennie Spring

One by one the rest of the students put down their papers. The shaft of sunlight on her desk moved off her pencil. Mrs. Fann stood up. Her lips began to form the letter P, for *pass your tests in.*

63

Janie penciled a wide harsh line through *Jennie Spring* and wrote, carefully, and in her very best script, *Janie Johnson.*

Middle school boys' basketball did not attract crowds.

The Spring family was the largest group there. There were nine more parents of basketball-team players and six cheerleader parents. An assortment of small children climbed precariously up and down the bleachers, or else sobbed with boredom and begged to be taken home. One mother had brought a box of Nilla cookies which she tossed like tiny Frisbees to any child in need of distraction. Half the cookies fell between the bleachers, and two shrieking, pummeling little boys raced around under them, joyfully licking up the crumbs.

Janie had forgotten, from the lofty view of tenth grade, just how pathetic sixth- and seventh-grade players could be. Twice, the "crowd" cringed, expecting a player to head the wrong way down the court and make a basket for the opposition. Twice, leaping, shouting, fist-gesturing coaches managed to stop them. Once, that boy was Brian.

Brendan played well and was in for most of the game. Brian played lousily and was on the bench for most of the game. It was not a comfortable sight for the family. The boys were used to being equal; they came in a set and always ended up in one.

Brendan's game total was a marvelous twenty-one points. He was slapping backs and laughing wildly, and yet struggling to be blasé.

Brian was finally put back in the game in the

last one and a half minutes of the fourth quarter. Then he played badly. He tripped, as if even his feet were tied up with frustration, embarrassment, and jealousy.

I'm a twin, thought Janie. Janie and Jennie. Twins. Sometimes I'm the good twin, with double-digit scores and people whistling. Sometimes I'm the bad twin, hardly able to remember who's on my team.

During a time-out, she accepted three quarters from Mrs. Spring to plunk in the vending machine out in the hallway for a soda. She and Jodie and Stephen went together out of the gym to get drinks.

They waited for Janie to get her soda first. When Jodie had her Sprite, she said brightly, "So. How was your day, Jennie?"

Be the good twin, Janie told herself. "Fine," she said.

Stephen dropped his quarters in and hit the root beer button like a punching bag.

"How was yours?" said Janie quickly to her sister.

"Terrific. I got a ninety-two in Japanese."

Janie stared at her sister. *"Japanese?"* she repeated.

"Yup. Only eleven of us are in third-year Japanese. Everybody else dropped out along the way. It's a very very hard language. We have nothing but contempt and scorn for people taking mere French or Spanish."

"You're taking Japanese?" repeated Janie. She was amazed and impressed. Somehow it didn't seem like Jodie.

"If you had ever looked across the bedroom when Jodie was doing her homework," said Stephen acidly, "you would have noticed she wasn't using an alphabet."

I hate him, thought Janie. She gripped the sweating, cold soda can and went back to the gym. Doesn't he realize how hard this is for me? she thought furiously.

The good-twin half of her thought: *It's hard for him, too.*

She climbed up next to Mrs. Spring again. Stephen wouldn't say anything in front of his mother.

We're both protecting our mothers, thought Janie.

In her purse were photographs of Mommy and Daddy. She could open the clasp, unzip the pocket, and shuffle through the familiar, beloved photos of her Connecticut mother and father. But already she did not want to hurt Mr. and Mrs. Spring's feelings by doing that.

What about Mommy and Daddy's feelings? she thought.

She did not unzip her purse, but felt the edge of the stack of photographs through the thin leather, playing with the corner as if it were a baby's pacifier.

What normal, decent person swaps families as easily as a pair of ice skates? she thought. It was evil of me to do it when I was three, but isn't it more evil of me to do it now that I am fifteen?

I bet I'm the kind of person who becomes a mass murderer. A sniper from a hotel balcony. A poisoner of public water supplies.

Everybody in this family—well, everybody but Stephen—is nice. Yet all I want to do is hurt them.

Was this just pouting and whining, like the three-year-old who had left them twelve years ago, or was she standing up for something right and true?

We need to talk, thought Janie. But I can't. I just can't. I can't bear the thought of talking. Unless it's to Mommy, or Daddy, or Reeve.

Jodie ached for her little brothers. She could tell by their expressions that they did not know what to do about being on different levels. Would they let it pass or dwell on it? Fight? Separate? Forget it? Maybe Brian would actually quit the team, leaving Brendan on his own—a first in their twinny lives.

Now that she shared a bedroom with somebody who did not want to share with her, she no longer envied twins.

How will they ever untwine? she thought, her heart breaking for both of them.

Maybe she could have a real conversation with Jennie about this. Maybe they could get into their feelings at last if they talked about the twins' feelings.

It made Jodie so nervous to address Jennie. Jennie took every sentence as something to deliberate, to weigh, and possibly to throw back. And now she had Stephen hanging over her shoulder, listening in, so that even if she made one syllable of progress, like Jennie being impressed about the Japanese, Stephen would ruin it. "Brian must be dying inside," Jodie said to her new sister.

Jennie nodded. "I would be."

Like a family, they watched Brian struggle while Brendan sat triumphant on the bench—most valuable player sitting out the last thirty seconds, having scored enough that it was now safe to put in the worst players. Such as his twin.

"Do you play basketball, Jennie?" asked Dad.

"No," said Jennie. "I don't like gym much. But Daddy coached soccer. He loves soccer. We went to all his games, of course."

The Daddy who had asked her the question did not ask any more.

What is the matter with her? thought Jodie. Why is she so cruel?

At the end of the game, Jennie headed straight for the car, forgetting they had to wait for the twins to shower and change. Forgetting, Jodie could only suppose, that she was related to those twins.

"What are we going to do about her, Dad?" said Jodie.

Jennie stood at the far end of the lobby, her back to them, waiting for them to catch up, but not turning to see what was taking them so long.

"We have to accept that this will take time," said her father.

"Don't push her," said Mom. But Mom looked after Jennie with such pain and longing that Jodie found herself wanting to get violent; beat Jennie's brains out in order to make her hug Mom and call Dad Dad.

Dad walked after Jennie. As he drew near his

daughter, Jodie's heart flipped over. The resemblance was clear all the way down the hall. The hair, the tilt of the head, the stance. She was so completely Dad's child. Did she know? Could she see it? If those Connecticut parents saw Dad and Jennie together, would they see it?

Jodie watched them talk. Because they *were* talking. Even Jennie. Say good things, Jodie willed. Be nice to Dad.

The team was out of the locker room as if they had spent no more than a split second in the shower. As Brendan came close, Jodie knew that this was in fact the case. She also knew that Jennie's family would never do anything as tacky as sweat too much and then skip showering.

Since the boys had won because of Brendan's playing, a celebration was called for. "Pizza Hut?" yelled the coach. "Everybody's going? Meet you there?"

Kids shouted yes, parents shouted maybe.

Jodie, Stephen, and Mom caught up to Dad and Jennie. Brendan the victor bounced and yelled among his teammates, far too excited with his victory to think of anything like family, or Jennie.

Brian hung back. "So, Jennie," he said to his sister, "did you enjoy the game?"

She smiled at him. "I wish you'd been put in more, Brian," she said, and the Spring family relaxed in unison.

Brian shrugged. "I'm not so hot. He was right not to put me in."

"Maybe the coach plays favorites," said Jennie, giving his pride an out.

"No," confessed Brian. His eyes fastened with pain on his twin. "I'm lousy."

Jennie touched him. Gently she put her hand on his shoulder to offer comfort. It was her first physical gesture toward any of them. Jodie had tears in her eyes. Dad was right. They couldn't push. They had to let Jennie have all the time she needed.

Twelve years wasn't an afternoon, after all. They couldn't expect the Johnsons' influence to dissolve the first month.

"What kind of pizza do you like, Jennie?" said Mom. "We'll get two extra-larges and each half different. So we usually order one half cheese, another half pepperoni, one half hamburger, and the last half everything, but you may pick a half."

"We don't eat pizza," said Jennie. "My mother doesn't believe in junk food."

What I'd like to do right now, thought Jodie, is shove her right in that pizza oven. Toast her nasty little personality.

Janie knew perfectly well what her real mother would say if she had witnessed this scene. *Did I bring you up to behave like this? I believe in manners! I believe in being nice! I believe in being thoughtful! What is the matter with you? Am I proud of you? No. I am not. Now be nice.*

Last winter, when she finally knew the truth, she had resolved never to reveal it. She would be Janie Johnson with all her heart and mind and soul. But she could not sustain the lie. She had told.

To make this work, she would have to put Janie Johnson away. To become Jennie Spring with all her heart and mind and soul.

But that too was a lie. And she was resisting with every molecule of energy she possessed. Every time she took a step forward—being nice to Brian— she took two back—pointing out as clearly and viciously as she could that her *real* family wasn't in New Jersey, her *real* family ate better, her *real* father was the one she called Daddy. So there!

As if the Springs were responsible for this.

As if the Springs had kidnapped her and not Hannah.

When the day finally ended, when the lights were finally turned out, Janie pulled the covers over her head in the room she shared with a stranger, buried her face in a pillow that didn't have the right texture or the right smell, and silently wept.

She woke up crying. It was not very late. Eleven-thirty. Janie wrapped herself in a bathrobe and went down the hall.

Mr. and Mrs. Spring were in the kitchen, drinking something hot.

"Hello, sweetie," said Mr. Spring.

Janie tried to smile at him. She couldn't. She said, "Would you let me telephone my mother?" She burst into tears the minute she said it.

"Oh, honey," said Mrs. Spring, "you're not a prisoner here, Jennie. I know it's a big change. I know you're scared. We're all scared. Of course you may telephone Mrs. Johnson."

Janie dialed Connecticut. Her mother said hello

grumpily. She was probably already in bed. "Mom? Mommy?" said Janie, and burst into tears again.

"Hello, darling," said her mother, crying at her end.

"Mommy!" said Janie again, and couldn't go on. She could not say *I want to come home*, not out loud, not with this other set of parents listening. The Springs' feelings were out on the table, like their mugs of tea or coffee.

But her mother had always understood everything. "It's hard, isn't it, sweetie?" said her mother. "Daddy and I have had a rough time. I'm so glad you called. It's wonderful to hear your voice."

"You haven't really heard my voice," said Janie. "All I said was Mom."

"My favorite word," said her mother.

Janie could not talk, so her mother did. Talked about her day, how she went to do her usual volunteer work and somehow lived through it. How Reeve had come over for a piece of cake and how awkward it had been. How Reeve wanted to telephone her, but it was agreed that she had to learn to swim by getting thrown into cold water.

"What does that mean anyway?" said Janie. It sounded like a bunch of people standing around watching somebody drown.

"You have a new family," said her mother. "I know there must be a million big adjustments."

Janie could not begin to list the adjustments. Especially not when the two biggest adjustments were sitting there.

"It has to work, darling," said her mother. "And that means we have to do our share of work, too. My work is not driving down there and getting you. Daddy's work is not re-kidnapping you and taking us to Mexico to live happily ever after. Your work is getting to know your new family and doing your best in your new school and figuring out how to be Jennie Spring."

"I don't want to," said Janie. Forbidden sentences rang like steeple bells in her head. *Would you come and get me? If I need you, would you re-kidnap me? Are you going to leave me here with these strangers?*

But she and her mother and father had been through that. They were not going to come. They were not her parents. They had no rights. They were surrendering her for good.

"I love you, Mommy," she said. She couldn't help it. No matter how much it hurt Mrs. Spring's feelings. Maybe they would be willing to work out a weekend thing, like a divorce. On alternate weekends, she could stay with her real parents.

Mr. Spring said, "Jennie? May I speak to Mrs. Johnson?"

She could hardly let go of the telephone. What if Mr. Spring made things worse? What if he told Janie's mother to butt out?

"We're not the enemy, Jennie," said Mr. Spring with a depth of sadness in his voice that matched her . . .

. . . her other father's.

She gave him the phone.

Mr. Spring chatted in a forced way. He said that Jennie was doing fine, but everybody knew adjustment would come hard and slow. He said that although they had agreed there would be no contact until Jennie had settled in, that was not going to work. "I think she needs to talk to you every day for a while. Then it can taper off."

Janie's heart was flying. She had a lifeline now. When she could not manage any longer, she could pick up the phone and hear the voices that mattered.

Finally she got the phone back. "Sweetie," said her mother, breathless with pleasure, "this is so wonderful. He sounds like a good father, Janie. He loves you, so does she, they're on your team. They're ready to make compromises. So you make some, too. Okay?"

"Okay." Then she talked to Daddy a little. He was gearing up for income-tax season. Lots of work to do, which was good, he needed to stay busy. "I love you, Janie," he whispered.

"I love you, too, Daddy," she said.

She forgot there was another Daddy in the room. When she hung up, almost caressing the telephone that she could now use, her New Jersey Dad was gripping his mug so hard she expected him to crush it, like a soda can. She had no idea what to say. She only knew that she felt so much better, so much more able to face tomorrow. She was actually able to smile at these people to whom she was related. "Good night," she said. "And—um—thank you."

Her father struggled to return the smile and didn't make it.

"Good night," said her mother, managing an expression that was half sob and half smile.

They are good people, she thought. They are my parents. They are on my team. I could love them if I tried.

Janie fled the hurricane of emotion, feeling her way in the dark bedroom, tucking herself deep under the covers.

And once more she could not sleep. A new nightmare surfaced. She did not have enough love to go around. Whatever love she gave these parents, she would have to take away from the others.

CHAPTER
9

School passed for Janie.

She found the library. The librarian was different from good old Mr. Yampolski back at her real school. This librarian was more like a prison warden of old dead books than an eager, knowledge-thirsty shouter and sharer like Mr. Yampolski.

She needed books. Since Jodie could sleep with the lights on, Janie would read into the night, keeping nightmares at bay. Her dreams were of falling. The cliff she clung to crumbled and everything around her was bottomless. Dark and slippery with the grime of evil. She would wake up drenched with sweat in the tight little bedroom, only a few feet separating her from the new sister whom she could not enjoy, and who definitely did not enjoy her.

Be nice, Janie ordered herself every morning, each time she faced one of her family, each time she needed to speak with them. She managed this not even half the time. The rest of the time, purposely, she was rotten.

The matter of the telephone was always difficult. The Springs could not afford long-distance calls. But Janie's real parents had given her permission to use their credit-card number any time she wanted. She could just go in the kitchen and poke in a thousand digits and speak to her parents. But she could not do it privately. This family did not know what privacy was. The only other phone was in Mr. and Mrs. Spring's bedroom, and Janie would have felt like a housebreaker going in there.

She was never left alone. Mr. and Mrs. Spring did not get home from work until late afternoon. Jodie and Stephen were virtually on rotation duty, making sure their new sister was always escorted, and safely locked indoors. Who did they think would kidnap her now?

Jodie was given to flashes of temper that vanished as quickly as they came. Janie rather envied this trait. It must be nice to be mad and be done.

Tired of romance and mystery novels, Janie found the rack of college catalogs and took some of them home. Janie had never wanted to go away to college. How terrifying those huge dorms full of strangers looked. Now she yearned for college because college had no parents. You did not have to divide your loyalties between the Connecticut parents you loved and the New Jersey parents you still could not believe were yours. College had no brothers and sisters either. If you didn't like your roommate, you could trade.

But the days became weeks, and what had been alien became ordinary.

The name of the beauty shop was Scissors, and outside in front hung an immense wooden pair of scissors, painted silver, glittering in the thin after-noon sun.

Mrs. Spring was the kind of person who was never happy at how her hair turned out and changed hairdressers continually. "Hairdressers hate Mom," Jodie informed her sister. "She hardly tips at all and then she goes to somebody else for exactly the same cut. So she can never go back a second time to anybody."

"I'm running out of options," said Mrs. Spring. "Pretty soon I'll have to go out of state for a trim."

"When did you have it cut last?" asked Janie. Mrs. Spring's hair was fluffy and ill-kempt. Her real mother, elegant and perfect, never had a hair out of place. And yet Janie felt a touch of affection for Mrs. Spring because her hair was a mess.

"Eight weeks ago," said Mrs. Spring. "Or ten. Or twenty."

"Twenty?" repeated Janie, laughing. "That's four or five months." Her real mother went every six weeks.

"Well, it gives me a chance to see if the beauti-cian knows how to deal with disaster."

Scissors was exactly like any hairdresser's Janie had been in. The same perfumed air, the same shampoo-y scent. The same rows of wet-haired women without makeup, smiling at their yet-to-be-made-pretty selves in the huge mirrors. Even the same beauticians: two incredibly thin girls with strange and impressive hair; a heavyset matron fresh from her cigarette break, her hair dyed an im-possible blond; and an amused young man, not surprisingly named Michael. The familiarity was soothing.

While they waited, Janie chose *Cosmopolitan;* this was no doctor's office where the only choice of reading material was *National Geographic* or *Sports Illustrated.* She and Jodie examined the cover for some time, wondering how the model had been laced into her bizarre gold gown.

"Three? Trims all around?" said the heavy beautician, bored. "I only got two on the schedule but we could fit the third in."

Fit in.

I could fit in, thought Janie, touching the wilderness of her hair. I could get this cut. It would make me more Jennie and less Janie. "Okay," she said. "Cut mine like"— she felt like a dentist extracting the word—"like my sister's."

"No!" shrieked Jodie, blocking the hairdresser as if she were armed. "You'd look terrible, Jennie. This isn't your cut. You have such beautiful hair." Jodie said to the hairdresser, "Absolutely not. Don't touch a hair on her head." She turned back to Janie. "See, I hardly have any hair. I have to cut it pixie like this because I am not hair-endowed. You, on the other hand, have to display your hair the way the *Cosmo* model displays her cleavage."

They giggled.

Like sisters.

Mrs. Spring and Jodie went in the back to be shampooed. Janie finished the magazine.

It's happening, she thought. Everybody told me that all it would take is time. Time alone. Days passing would turn me into Jennie Spring.

79

She stared at her watch. How incredible that time—invisible, lost-forever time—marked by little changing hands on a tiny decorated circle, could change her family, her name, and her thoughts.

I can lean into it, thought Janie. I can take this turn in the road. Become a Spring. Or I can step back.

"You can't play?" said Jodie, as if Janie had said she couldn't speak English. "I'll teach you. You'll love it. It's very addictive. We're crazy about it." She handed Janie a joystick. Janie had played plenty of computer games, of course, just not Super Mario. She and Stephen and Jodie sat on the edge of the couch staring at the TV screen.

It took her a while to figure out how to make Mario fly and swim and bounce high enough. Janie was determined to keep up, but it was impossible; Stephen and Jodie had mastered the game ages ago and were wonderful.

When Stephen played, he sat completely still, eyes riveted on the screen, moving nothing but his fingertips.

Jodie, however, played sitting on the edge of her chair. She looked like the top half of a ballet dancer. Her legs and feet lay still, but her arms curled and leaped as she lifted Mario up a cliff. She sank down into her own lap when Mario slid on an ice floe and she rotated herself desperately as she tried to hurl Mario over boiling lava. Janie loved watching her. Jodie was a remarkably unselfconscious person in play and in sleep: thrashing and moving and making faces.

Before long, Janie was in the Vanilla Dome, tucking under safe overhangs to escape blue-bubbled enemies. Just when she thought she was going to make it, blue bubbles came from both directions. "Oh, no!" shrieked Janie, trying frantically to run. "I'm dead! I have no hope! Look what's coming!"

Sure enough, Janie was killed, and the cheerful *that's-it-for-you!* music took her off the screen.

Jodie giggled. "You sounded like a pilot being shot down in World War Two. 'Oh, no! I have no hope!'"

"How many lives do you have left?" asked Stephen.

"Just one."

"Hah!" said Jodie with satisfaction. "I have twenty-two."

Janie studied their play, memorizing the tricks and keys. She had memorized the little Nintendo songs without meaning to, the way you memorized the theme to *Jeopardy.* They sang in her head, like little companions.

"Let's get something to eat," said Stephen.

Mesmerized by the game, Janie hated to pause it just so they could eat. Jodie laughed at her. "Your stomach is growling, you need a snack so much."

It was true.

"The game sucks you in, doesn't it?" said Jodie. "There's never a time when you're really ready to stop."

"Yes, there is," said Stephen. "All of a sudden you're so sick of it you can't believe you've spent the whole day there."

"Don't tell Mom and Dad we played two solid

hours, Jennie," cautioned Jodie, following her brother into the kitchen. "And especially don't tell them you died fifty times," she yelled back. "They think all that dying makes you callous and perverted. They might even take the Nintendo away."

Stephen and Jodie discussed snack possibilities. They decided to stick chocolate chip cookies under the broiler to melt the chips. Neat idea, thought Janie, getting up and going after them. Daddy would love that.

Daddy.

The cozy school-day afternoon died as if Janie had put a knife through it. She had actually forgotten Mommy and Daddy. She had been having fun. She had liked being in this house, with this brother and sister. For an entire afternoon, she had put her parents on the shelf of her mind, storing them for backup.

Mommy and Daddy will shift into the past, she thought. Soon they will be shadows. People I remember in slow moments, or sad times.

No!

That's not what I want!

I said I'd try—but I didn't want it to work!

"Cookies are ready!" yelled Stephen.

"I don't want any," said Janie. She felt herself stiffening, as if she were preparing for war.

Jodie popped back into the living room. "Yes, you do. Come on. I just poured milk."

"I am allergic to milk," said Janie sharply. "How many times do I have to tell you that?" Stop it, she told herself, don't pick a fight.

Jodie stared. "Why don't you come on in and

tell us again, Jennie?" she said. "We're slow learners, we Springs. Anyway, we love hearing about you and the Johnsons. About how you never have pizza and you're always going horseback riding and you need a thirtieth Swatch."

Janie walked past. If they had a fight, it would exonerate her from forgetting about the Johnsons. Her loyalties twisted and swung, like a dead person hung from a tree. She opened the refrigerator door roughly and pushed the available drinks around.

"Don't like our selection?" said Jodie hotly. "Wish you were in a better-stocked kitchen? Up there in Connecticut where they do things right?"

"Yes!" snapped Janie.

Stephen lifted the plate of hot cookies between their snarling faces. The rich aroma of hot chocolate interfered with the fight. "Come on, Jennie. Come on, Jo. Dad told us to get along. So get along."

"She isn't trying," said Jodie.

"She was for a while. Two hours is the most we can expect of her."

Janie stiffened.

Stephen waved the plate on a slant. "Dig in. Your big brother's very own homemade cookies."

If I had grown up here, Janie thought, would I idolize Stephen? Would this be the big brother I leaned on for advice? Would I think he was a wonderful guy and would my girlfriends want to date him?

She leaned on the huge white refrigerator, wishing she could lean on Reeve, or Mommy, or Daddy. Anything but this place.

Jodie actually picked up a kitchen chair and flung it.

Janie leapt out of the way even though the chair came nowhere near her.

"I hate you!" Jodie screamed, eyes blazing. Jodie grabbed the plate out of Stephen's hands and threw that, too. Chocolate splatted where it hit the kitchen wall. "You can't even take a cookie from us! You have brought nothing to this family but hurt and pain. Since you were three years old." Jodie began sobbing. "I thought you would be so much fun. I always wanted a sister. And we were named to go together. Jodie and Jennie." Jodie wiped her eyes and went on screaming. "I thought we'd share clothes and giggle and tell stories like a slumber party. But you'd rather lie there in the dark like a stick or read a book. You can't stand talking to me. And you write your other name on your homework and you telephone those people all the time."

She was right and Janie knew it, but could not admit it. "They are not *those people*! They're my parents!" said Janie fiercely.

Stephen actually got between them.

"You might as well be stabbing Mom with a butcher knife the way you act, Jennie! You're not even trying," yelled Jodie. "I hate you! You're a mean, spoiled—" Jodie bit off the rest of her sentence.

Mr. and Mrs. Spring walked in, home from work and no doubt sorry. They stared incredulously at the dumped cookies and upside-down chair.

It's my fault, thought Janie. I wanted a fight. I practically choreographed a fight.

84

Mrs. Spring put a hand lightly on Janie's shoulder and the other hand not so lightly on Jodie's.

But she did not say anything. She did not take sides. She did not make some grown-up type statement about what this meant. She did not say what they were going to do next.

After a long time, Janie realized that Mrs. Spring did not know what to do next.

Nobody did.

CHAPTER
10

Reeve Shields had driven to New Jersey before.

That was when he was still practically a little kid. He'd been seventeen, so crazy about Janie that just being alone with her in his Jeep filled his entire mind. Not that being with Janie was ever a mind-thing. It was a body-thing. Thinking about his body and her body was so intoxicating that Reeve found his own body useless. Swallowing, breathing, gripping a steering wheel—difficult in Janie's presence.

He had lived next door to Janie ever since he could remember. You weren't supposed to fall in love with the girl next door; she was supposed to be too familiar and too ordinary.

But Janie, her slender but deeply curving shape, her silken but ridiculously fluffy shining red hair . . .

Reeve had his first college acceptance.

It was so amazing. He would not have thought there was a college in America that would want him. Reeve had spent freshman, sophomore, and junior years killing time and staring at girls. This did not produce high grades. This did not even produce homework. He had picked up steam senior year, but his grade average was definitely average.

He held the acceptance letter in his hand. Even the envelope was precious, with its college logo and return address. He loved knowing that his name and address were in their computer. They wanted him.

Reeve wanted to tell the world, but mostly he wanted to tell Janie.

You never saw lights on at her house now. The wide glass plates that filled the side wall of the Johnson house were dark. Mr. and Mrs. Johnson must sit in the dark, staring at the shadows, thinking their dark thoughts.

Janie had been their light.

Reeve did not understand why Janie had to be gone forever, why there could be no swapping or weekending, but the family in New Jersey had been firm. This is *our* daughter, they said. You didn't know you were stealing her, but you did. Your time is up. We're bringing her home. Do not interfere.

Even Reeve got his marching orders: do not interfere.

Settle in, that was the big phrase. Janie had to "settle in." Then Reeve might be allowed to get in touch with her. Might. Nothing was certain.

Janie had written him twice from school. Letters scribbled surreptitiously during class. Ripped from spiral notebooks, stamped and mailed by a girl named Chrissy who sat next to Janie in choir.

The whole thing was wrong. They were piling more secrets on a girl who could hold no more, and now she was adding secrets of her own. Reeve thought she might collapse under the weight of secrets.

He still saw Mr. and Mrs. Johnson going to work or out for dinner or bringing in groceries. They still called hello to him, and asked how school was going. But they never mentioned Janie.

He'd asked his mother why not.

"They don't want to break down," said his mother. "They can't start crying. They'd never stop."

"Does Mrs. Johnson talk to you about it?" Reeve wanted to know.

Girls talked so much more than boys. He had listened to Janie enough hours to know they needed talk more. It wasn't just the accumulating facts of her kidnapping that had overwhelmed Reeve, it was the number of times Janie needed to analyze them. Why wasn't once enough? Why did girls need to talk so much?

Reeve preferred action. Physical action. Every time he and Janie had been ready to move beyond kissing, it turned out that only he was ready; Janie was just ready for more talk.

There were times when he felt this was her master plan, to distract him.

Nothing had ever distracted Reeve from Janie's body.

But he was eighteen now, and had been accepted at college. He was in a different car-insurance category, and he could vote, and enter the army . . . and on a Saturday in March, he could drive to New Jersey with or without parental permission.

He wanted to flourish the letter in front of

Janie. See Janie's eyes light up. Hear Janie's cry of delight. He wanted Janie to wrap her arms around him, and tell him how brilliant he was, and what a magnificent future lay ahead of him.

Then he wanted to get in the Jeep and drive her to some secluded spot.

When it came to fantasies, he had had them all.

On the telephone, Caitlin said, "Maybe you could think of Jennie as an exchange student. You know. From Nigeria or Mongolia. And naturally she has different customs and different habits. And doesn't even speak your language. And so naturally she's homesick."

Cait was always sure of her psychology. She referred to herself as Jodie's best friend. And that might be true, but it was not what Jodie wanted. Jodie wanted her sister to be her best friend. "I guess I'm not mad at Jennie so much as I'm mad at myself," said Jodie. Think of her as an exchange student, she thought. It wasn't such a bad idea. No matter what Jennie's like, she promised herself, I'll be a diplomat. I will be the ambassador to Jennie's foreign country. "I shouldn't have yelled," said Jodie. "I should have hung on to my temper."

"Yes," agreed Cait. "You were a total jerk and lost everything you'd gained."

Best friends, thought Jodie, or sisters, don't call you a total jerk. They stick by you.

She wondered if she had either a best friend or a sister.

She got off the phone. She was too depressed to talk. That was depressed. She avoided her own room; Jennie was in there. She headed down to the playroom instead. When the phone rang in the kitchen, she didn't even race to the bottom of the stairs to see if it was for her.

"Mommy!" said Janie. She was so happy. Her mother had not once telephoned her; Janie had done all the calling home.

But it was not a happy call. "Sweetie, Frank and I have spent a long time on the phone with Mr. and Mrs. Spring."

Not "your father and I" but "Frank and I." Janie's heart clutched.

"Janie, this is the most terrible thing I have ever had to say. Please forgive me for saying it. I love you, and that's why I'm saying this. You are with your mother and father now. They seem like wonderful people, sweetheart. We knew they'd be. They're *your* parents after all. And they've told us everything. You're not trying, darling. You're not trying at all. I want you to try, honey."

Honey. Sweetheart. Darling. But not, and never again, Daughter.

"It's hard," said Janie, her throat filling up and her eyes overflowing.

"It's hard here, too." No mother is made of material tough enough to give away her baby without weeping.

"Does Daddy want me to try?"

Her mother sobbed once, and then her father came on the line. "Yes, honey, I want you to try," he said. "We brought you up. We brought you up to be good and decent and loving. Your mother believes in

90

helping others; she believes that the purpose of our being on earth. We tried to teach you that. And now the people you have to help are your own mother, your own father, your three brothers, and your sister."

"What if I love you better? What if I want to come home?"

"Ah, baby," said her father. "In this field of wrongs, there has to be a right somewhere. And it's right for you to be back with your real family."

Write your resolutions down, they said next. You always loved to keep special notebooks and diaries. Resolve that you're going to be a Spring.

Talk about blackmail, thought Janie resentfully. She was actually glad to say good-bye to Mommy and Daddy. Whose side were they on, anyway?

Alone—for once—in Jodie's bedroom, Janie got out the blue cloth three-ring binder. What they had been through together, she and this notebook! Lying inside was the flattened milk carton that had gotten her here. If only she had never stolen Sarah-Charlotte's milk. None of this would have happened.

Wouldn't they all be much happier? Even Mrs. Spring—wouldn't she be happier without this hostile enemy daughter in her home?

But that's what my parents mean, thought Janie Johnson. Stop being a hostile enemy daughter.

She opened the binder to a fresh page. The familiar white paper with the thin blue lines and red margin marker stared back. Connecticut, New Jersey, or California—they all used the same paper in school. One by one, she wrote, not New Year's Resolutions, but New Family Resolutions.

- I will call Mr. and Mrs. Spring Mom and Dad.
- When the Springs say, "Jennie?" I will answer instead of looking around as if I don't know who they're talking about.
- I will stop daydreaming that I am still Janie Johnson.
- I will fit in.
- I will not cry myself to sleep and I will not hide in the girls' room at school and cry there either.

Well, that seemed like enough. She should be able to break those resolutions in twenty-four hours or so.

Doing it was different.

This was the house around which Reeve and Janie had skulked when they were trying to figure out the milk-carton secret. Back when Janie was sure it was a fantasy created by her subconscious. But they had seen those red-haired twins get off the school bus and known: the milk carton told the truth.

Reeve parked the Jeep in the road.

His eighteenth year had turned him into a man. His arms and legs had thickened. Weight lifting and track, which he loved because the sports taxed him and because they were almost, but not quite, solitary, had come through for him. He could feel the impact of himself. He felt safer inside himself because of the size of his body and the power of his muscles. How awful Janie must feel, he suddenly thought, so light and fragile, a person whose position can be shifted by anybody stronger.

For a moment he didn't feel very strong either. Then he walked up and rang the bell. Harder than track. The front door opened. This had to be the oldest brother: Stephen. Also a senior, but a year younger than Reeve. Still skinny. Still a growing boy.

How Reeve used to hate that phrase. He got it a lot at Christmas when relatives materialized. My, you're a growing boy! Grown now, he thought gladly. "Hi," he said, extending his hand. "You must be Stephen. I'm Reeve Shields. Janie's boyfriend."

Stephen, slightly stunned, let him in. Reeve was in luck—or out of it, depending on what happened next: the parents were right there. Reeve introduced himself to Mr. and Mrs. Spring.

"You're the young man who drove her down here last fall," said Mr. Spring. "Have a seat. Hungry?"

Reeve, who was always hungry, liked him immediately and was surprised. He had cast Mr. and Mrs. Spring as The Enemy. Mr. Spring was an inch shorter than Reeve, which was nice. However, he was several inches broader in the shoulders and many pounds heavier. He had a beard that looked like nothing so much as Janie's hair pasted on his chin. Reeve could not imagine wanting that around your mouth and all over your throat.

But then, Reeve was new enough to shaving that he still thought standing in front of that mirror and using that razor was the best thing that had ever happened to him. Sex would be better, but sex was harder to get than razors. "Is Janie home?"

"Jennie," Mr. Spring corrected him. "Yes, she is."

"Yes, I am!" said Janie, coming into the room.

Reeve turned, and even though he knew how glad he would be to see her, still, he was amazed at how *very* glad he was to see her.

The sight of Janie Johnson made him laugh and want to throw things. All his life Reeve had reacted to good news and bad by wanting to throw things. It was a habit his parents had tried to end for years. Now he wanted to gather Janie in his arms and throw her in the air and catch her.

So he did.

11

The boy actually asked Dad's permission to take Jennie out for the rest of Saturday.

Jodie knew Dad didn't want to say yes, and also knew Dad didn't have grounds for refusing either. Dad had to confine himself to saying, "You have a five-hour drive to get home, don't you, Reeve?"

"Yes, sir." Jodie knew Dad would love that "sir." The boy even looked military, with that buzz cut and those broad shoulders.

"When do you need to leave in order to get home at a reasonable hour?"

The boy grinned. This is one good-looking guy, thought Jodie. No wonder Jennie isn't interested in anybody else! I should be so lucky!

The boy said, "Mom and Dad get pretty worked up if I'm not home by one A.M. on a Saturday."

"Then I guess you and my daughter had better be here by eight."

"Thanks," said the boy, heaving a huge sigh of relief.

Jodie was astonished. If Dad had said, "You can't take her anywhere," Reeve would have obeyed.

Jennie was dancing in circles around Reeve, using him like a ballerina's bar. Her fingertips traveled everywhere on his chest and back and arms. Jodie would not have recognized her.

This is the sister we want, thought Jodie. This thrilled, laughing, happy, giddy girl is Jennie. We haven't had this Jennie. She hasn't given us this.

Would Reeve's visit break the ice? Would Jennie come home able to laugh and dance and parade? Or would Jennie miss him so much when he left that she would get even more somber and quiet?

Was Jennie like this with her parents?

Parents.

Jodie caught the word in her mind. No letting herself think of Mr. and Mrs. Johnson as Jennie's parents.

Jodie watched through a slit in the front curtains as Reeve and Jennie went out to his Jeep. Reeve was big and solid. Jennie was small next to him, but a whirlwind—more energy in her this moment than in all the weeks she had lived with the Springs.

She's in love, thought Jodie, who had had crushes, but never what she would have considered true love. Jodie was waiting for love, thinking of it continually, hoping each new school day, dreaming before each new event, grieving every night, for true love had not yet arrived.

"She's in love," said Mom, looking out the same curtain opening.

Dad put his arms around Mom and hugged her hard. "So am I," he said, kissing her on the lips. They had tears in their eyes.

The Jeep drove away.

"She's so beautiful," whispered Mom.

Dad nodded. "At least we know what we're aiming for. That laugh. That eagerness. That energy."

"We won't get it," said Stephen. "She'll keep it for *them.*"

Janie had not forgotten she was in love with Reeve, but so many worries had interfered. So much new business. So many strangers.

The sight of him—so poised and at ease in the crowded living room, his dark complexion such a contrast to the fair, freckled faces of her new family —slugged her. Her boyfriend filled her whole horizon and her whole mind. "Reeve!" she shouted, although it came out a whisper.

Reeve was here. He had driven five hours, through New York City traffic, paying tolls, buying gas, and ignoring the orders of three sets of parents: his, hers, and her second pair.

To see me, she thought.

And Janie, in turn, saw nobody but Reeve. The long bones and strong muscles, the lean face and immense grin of the boy she had loved all winter but had had to put in second place. First place was the milk carton. How could a folded piece of cardboard be strong enough to open and close whole families?

"Reeve!" she said now, laughing wildly, unable to sit on her side of the Jeep, half in his lap, her kisses landing all over his face. They drove, not very safely. He had had a buzz. No more moppy sloppy hair to run her fingers through. She tickled her palm against his head.

"So how's the family?" said Reeve.

"We're not really a family," she said. "Or at least, I'm not. I guess I need family lessons."

Reeve did not smile. "I'm told it isn't lessons you need, Janie. Just a lot of practice."

"What!" She was furious. Had Reeve been sent on a parental mission to scold her? "Don't you get on my case, Reeve Shields! Do you know what I've been through?"

"I'm sorry. I do know. I just think you should have—"

"Well, maybe I should have! But I didn't. There isn't an etiquette book for my situation, Reeve Shields. I did the best I could." She had not done the best she could. She knew it, and certainly Jodie and Stephen knew it. Her cheeks went red keeping the secret.

Reeve put his hand over hers. "Don't call me both names. Reeve Shields. It sounds like my mother yelling at me."

Janie definitely did not want to sound like anybody's mother. She tightened her fingers around his and examined the brand-new class ring. He was turning eighteen, and I didn't so much as send him a card. He was applying to colleges, and I didn't even know what ones. I was thinking of ten hundred other things. There wasn't room in my head for anybody but—

—but myself.

The extent of her selfishness stretched to Connecticut.

"Janie," said Reeve hesitantly. "I've been thinking about—well—your real age."

"We're sticking with my fake age," said Janie.

He laughed and squeezed her hand. "I'm eighteen now and it turns out you're a whole year younger than we thought. You're *little*. You're just a little girl, Janie Johnson."

"Yeah, well, I can whip you, big guy."

"Oh, yeah, the way you used to whip me in tennis, huh?"

They both laughed. Janie had no arm strength. Just lifting the tennis racket wiped her out for the day, never mind hitting the ball over the net.

Reeve looked at her through his long lashes. When he had had long hair as well, every sideways look from Reeve had been flirty and adorable. Adorable just wasn't a word Janie could use with quarter-inch-high hair. But she still loved his lashes.

"Remember tennis lessons?" he said softly.

"How could I forget?"

"You know what else I could give you a lesson in?"

She knew the topic immediately. "On whom," she said, "have you been practicing?"

He just grinned. The grin went on and on until she had to deflect it. "Reeve, I've been so selfish since I came here!"

"I knew it," he said, flopping back against the seat. "I knew you would want to talk instead."

"I *was* selfish, though."

"I happen to love the self that you are. And I want to get to know it better. Lots, lots better."

She was starved for love. What a contradiction, considering that she had *two* families who loved her so much it put them all in agony.

What is love, anyway? thought Janie. "Reeve," she said, "what do you think love really is?"

"Love," said Reeve firmly, "does not involve talking."

They were back early. Jodie was surprised. But she was really surprised when Reeve stayed until eight o'clock, his deadline for the drive home. He wanted, he said, to get to know the family.

It should have been the most awkward evening of the year, but it was not. Everybody had fun. Reeve was a doll. Jodie was crazy about him. And she was crazy about the girl that Jennie was while Reeve sat next to her.

Reeve was somebody the twins would want to go camping with and Dad would want to work on cars with and Mom would love cooking for. Reeve was the kind of boy Jodie wanted herself.

Reeve even succeeded with Stephen. The physical contrast between the boys was major, but the contrast in confidence and experience was even greater. Reeve was the youngest in a big family, and his parents had obviously relaxed and let him go early. Stephen was the oldest in a big family, but nobody had ever relaxed here, and Stephen had not been let go for anything. Jodie saw her older brother suddenly as homebound, a little too young for his age. She hoped Stephen didn't see that. His anger would just get angrier.

"Mr. Spring?" said Reeve. For the first time he looked apprehensive.

"Yes?"

"I was wondering—I mean, I didn't ask the

Johnsons about this. Or my own parents. But I was . . ." Reeve looked fast and hot at Janie and then at the ceiling and then at Dad.

He wants to elope, thought Jodie, ready to giggle or applaud.

Everything poised and sure in the eighteen-year-old evaporated. He staggered through the next sentences like a four-year-old on his first bike. "It's my senior year and the senior prom is June second and I want to take Janie and I guess I need permission because I'd have to come get her and she'd have to stay the night, or maybe two nights, and I'm not sure—like—where she'd stay over, at night, that is, if you don't want her at Mr. and Mrs. Johnson's, but they're great people, except she could stay at my house, my parents would love that—but—well, what I'm asking is—"

"Sure," said Jodie's father, grinning.

Reeve stopped floundering. "She can come to the prom?"

Dad nodded. "Of course she can. She'll have a wonderful time."

"I can?" cried Janie. "Really? You'll let me? You'll let me go to Reeve's prom?"

"Yes," said Dad.

Jodie did clap. "Ooooh, we can shop for a prom gown! I've always wanted to shop for prom gowns." She got permission all around. "Can't we, Mom? Can we, Jennie? Can we buy a prom gown with you?"

Jennie was crying.

"Don't cry!" said Reeve, making a terrible face

and shaking Jennie's sleeve. "I hate crying," he said to Mr. Spring, as if they were buddies.

"It does get old," agreed Mr. Spring.

"She isn't *crying*-crying," said Jodie. "She's happy-crying."

Janie agreed, nodding like a sister. She smiled at Jodie, who felt as if she had just won a thousand dollars. "Prom shopping. It'll be great."

"That's what matters? That's what this is about?" said Reeve. "Dresses?"

"Did you think it was about love or something?" said Dad.

The trembling expression between Janie and Reeve was explicit; clearly, they had thought it was about love or something.

Jodie tried to imagine Mom sitting down with Jennie to talk about Safe Sex or (much more likely from Mom) No Sex. It might be late for that, or it might not. Jodie couldn't tell. She wished Jennie would tell her tonight, but doubted it would happen. Still, they'd shared something good. They'd been sisters there for a moment.

The kiss Reeve and Jennie exchanged when they parted was almost chaste. They were intoxicated by seeing where they had touched, but mostly thinking of where they had not.

"Wow," muttered Stephen.

They watched their sister watching her boyfriend go.

And the great good gift that Reeve left behind was that when Jennie turned around, she was still smiling. And she kept smiling.

* * *

Reeve could not wait to tell Mr. and Mrs. Johnson how wonderful Janie had looked, what a great time they had had together, how terrific Mr. Spring had been about the prom, what fun the whole family was.

First thing Sunday morning he crashed into the Johnson house, the way he always had, and Mrs. Johnson offered him French toast, the way she always did, and Reeve accepted of course, because only mental cases turned down Mrs. Johnson's food.

"Janie looks fabulous," he told them. "We had the greatest day!" He recounted every moment except of course the one that counted: the one between himself and Janie.

It never occurred to him when he bounded out of the house, full of plans for proms and visits, that Mrs. Johnson wept again. But this time, for the daughter who could be happy in another mother's home.

12

How much easier to follow rules when she'd been ordered to! And maybe easier, too, because they were written down, and Janie could refer to them, like commandments.

But mostly it was easier because she had Reeve again. His visit stayed with her, encircling her like some wonderful twenty-first-century weapon. She could say his name, like a talisman, and be swept up into the same delight she'd felt when his presence slugged her there in the Springs' living room. She could look around the high school that had overwhelmed her so badly and see interesting people who posed no threats. She could relax again.

The unlikable qualities of this family had been her problem. She'd been as prickly as a porcupine. When they got mad, she held them responsible, not herself. She counted the days of her goodness: Saturday (Reeve Day), Sunday, Monday, Tuesday, Wednesday, Thursday.

Mrs. Spring—she could not yet say Mom—was actually kind of fun. Mr. Spring—whom she had come very close to calling Dad—was definitely fun.

He was forever concerned that his kids would be limp, useless couch potatoes and insisted on family exercise, like Rollerblading. Like somebody rolling socks, Mr. Spring pushed at his family to make them move.

Brendan and Brian turned out to be nice kids. Maybe a little dull. A quality of being wrapped up in each other that she had never run into before. Their brand of twinness was interesting to watch, but nothing she coveted. Stephen turned out not to be sulky, just sharp-edged.

Jodie was harder, maybe because the two girls were together so much more. And yet Jodie seemed worth more than any of the boys. Every now and then Janie knew they were sisters; she could feel the bond of it and it was surprisingly precious.

"There's a school dance next week," said Jodie. "Let's go. We'll stick together. You'll have a good time."

Janie loved dancing. She could let go with her body the way she could never let go with speech. She loved being in a big gym or cafeteria, the DJ turning the volume up high—higher!—highest!—until the drums seemed to be living in her heart. "But won't you each have a date?" she said.

Stephen looked horrified.

Janie had to laugh. "If that isn't typical," she said. "Reeve used to look like that when you mentioned girls. He'd gag all over the floor, and pretend to go into violent convulsions, and maybe die of some terrible poison."

"When was that?" said Jodie. "Not recently."

"When we were in junior high."

105

"Were you in love with him when you were in junior high?"

"Get real," said Janie. "When I was in junior high, I thought boys should live in a zoo and have keepers."

"Wait'll you go to a dance here," said her sister. "You'll still think that."

The bus jerked violently to a stop. They had forgotten they were even on the school bus, let alone jammed three in a two-person seat. Now Stephen remembered his resentment at not being offered a car ride home. Jodie remembered the weight of the homework. Janie wondered if there would be a card from Reeve. He had discovered Hallmark. He had sent her a card a day for five lovely days.

It was remarkable how soul-restoring a piece of mail—a funny greeting card—could be. Maybe I should send Mommy and Daddy cards, Janie thought. But even Hallmark won't observe *my* special occasion.

Janie got off the bus first. Up and down Highview Avenue were signs of spring. Red buds on twigs. Daffodils emerging. Southern New Jersey got spring earlier than Connecticut. Good. Because spring was more romantic than winter.

Stephen jabbed Jodie in the ribs and pointed.

The driveway was full of cars. Mom's. Dad's. The one that had to be Mr. Mollison's. Two Jodie did not recognize by driver, but easily recognized by model. State troopers' unmarked souped-up sedans.

Slowly they followed Jennie off the bus.

106

How would she handle this? What would happen now?

Brendan and Brian were leaping around on the sidewalk, belting each other, having gotten off the middle-school bus moments earlier.

"Don't you have practice?" snapped Jodie.

"Canceled. Anyway, we didn't want to miss the fireworks."

"What fireworks?" asked Jennie.

"Mr. Mollison is here," said Brendan, jabbing the air like a boxer.

Mr. Mollison had gotten a new car, of course. Jodie would have recognized the old one. He had probably had several new cars in the years since they had seen each other. For a while, Mr. Mollison had almost been a member of the family. There he was now, in the picture window, waiting for them to come in. He waved. Jodie did not wave back.

"Who is Mr. Mollison?" Jennie asked.

I want to be your sister, thought Jodie, not the person who tells you who Mr. Mollison is. And definitely not the person who tells you what he is going to do.

CHAPTER

13

The living room and the dining L of the Springs' house shared a long, windowless wall. The couch was pressed up against the living-room end and the sideboard against the dining-room end. The wall above the couch was completely covered with framed photographs of the children. One was the picture that had found its ultimate use on a milk carton.

It showed a laughing toddler, bright red hair yanked into pigtails high on each side of her head. Her dress—the famous summertime dress—was white with vivid dark polka dots.

She wanted to run, but the Spring family blocked the stairs and the hallway. Police filled the chairs. Janie could not seem to hear what the police were saying to her, nor find the vocabulary to answer them. Her head spun around as if it were popping off, the way Barbie-doll heads popped off if you dressed them too hard.

"Let's sit down, Jennie," said the biggest policeman. He held out his hands as if to show her that they were empty, that he held no weapon.

She wanted her mother, the one who had loved her and brought her up. But of course it was her New Jersey mother who crossed the carpet, circled the coffee table, and tried to touch her. Janie backed away. She could not back any farther. The room was not large enough.

The world was not large enough. How was she supposed to stay loyal to Mommy and Daddy during this? But she had promised to keep her Family Resolutions, too. What would the police find out in this interrogation? Janie did not want to know one single thing more than she already knew.

"There's nothing to be afraid of, Jennie," said the policeman. "We just want to talk. Nobody is going to get hurt."

"Do my parents know about this?" she said. "Are they okay?"

"We've talked to your parents." He knew she meant the Connecticut ones. "They're okay."

They were not okay. They had not been okay since the news broke. How could she trust a person who lied like that?

The policeman said softly to the Springs, "I think we might do better if all of you went into another room, okay? This is going to be hard on everybody and maybe we could talk a little easier without you."

"I'm her father," said Mr. Spring, "and I'm not leaving."

Janie stared at that big, tired red-bearded man. He seemed alternately and both family and stranger. Her Connecticut father would not have left the room either. He is a father, thought Janie. And I guess he's mine. "They can stay." She felt behind her, finding the arm and lowering herself into the corner of the sofa. One of those awkward pillows that serve no purpose made a lump behind her back. She picked it up. It was soft and velvety in her arms, and she held it against her chest like a teddy bear or a shield.

"I'm Mr. Mollison," said the policeman. She had a feeling he had told her that several times. This time she could hear him. "I'm the FBI officer who was assigned to your case twelve years ago, Jennie. And this is Mr. Fabrioli, who is with the state police, and Mr. Saychek, from the local police. Each of us is doing different things now, but we've come back to help on the Jennie Spring case since we're the most familiar with it."

I'm not her. I stopped being her twelve years ago.

Jodie could hardly bear to look at her sister.

Jennie's fingers scrabbled around the pillow like little separate animals trying to hide under leaves. Her eyes darted around the room looking for a safety zone. Her speech pattern changed radically. With every sentence she sounded younger and younger, as if she were falling backward in time, to when she was three years old, and by the end of the interview they would actually hear the three-year-old's version.

Jodie's mother tried to stifle tears. The weeping had nothing to do with the kidnapping. Mom was weeping because she could not hold this daughter in her arms to comfort or protect her. Jennie would crawl under the sofa first.

It took Mr. Mollison several more minutes of talking, and then he was the one who sat down next to Jennie. He was able to put his arm around her shoulder and get her to talk. Jennie talked only to him. The Spring family might as well not have been there at all.

"Jennie," said Mr. Mollison. He had a big, slow voice, as if they had all day; would always have all day. "We don't want to talk about what we think happened, but only the things you really remember."

"I don't remember," said Jennie quickly.

Mr. Mollison nodded for a while. Then he said, "Must have been pretty scary to pick up that milk carton in the school cafeteria and recognize your own picture on it."

Jennie clutched the pillow even harder.

"Did you say anything to the kids you were eating with?" asked Mr. Mollison.

"I said I was the face," said Jennie. "Out loud. Right away."

"And what did your friends say to that?" asked Mr. Mollison.

"They said I must really want to get out of the math test," said Jennie.

Jodie had to laugh.

Jennie let go of the pillow a little. "No, wait," she said. "I wasn't the one with the math test. Pete and Adair had the math test. I was going to have to read my English essay out loud. See? I've already gotten the facts wrong. You can't use me for facts. I get them mixed up. See?"

"It's easy to mix things up," agreed Mr. Mollison, smiling. His big torso nodded along with his head, and he and Jennie almost rocked together. "You must have figured whoever put that photograph on the milk carton was pretty mixed up, too."

Jennie nodded. "Because my parents were my parents. And they're good. See, I had my whole childhood. I was there. I lived it. And kidnapping is wrong. It's evil. Only terrible people would do that." Her chin was dimpling in and out as she fought sobbing. "And my parents are good. So I knew that it wasn't really my picture on there."

"And yet . . ." said Mr. Mollison. "You took the milk carton home that day, didn't you?"

Jennie clung to the pillow again. "Just in case," she said.

Jodie remembered the day Mom and Dad had decided to put Jennie's picture on the milk cartons. Talk about arguments!

Uncle Paul said absolutely categorically *not* to; it would just put everybody through it all over again. The baby had been killed and they had accepted that fact years ago. Why drag up something so hopeless and futile yet again?

Aunt Luellen said, "This is ridiculous. Nobody could recognize a teenage girl from a picture of her when she was three!" Aunt Luellen whipped out pictures of Stephen and Jodie when they were three, and sure enough, they were generic, assembly-line tots, not a single thing about them that carried into their teenage photographs.

Neighbors who had lived there when Jennie vanished said not to do it; the Springs would get phony calls from crazies and go through yet more hell. Neighbors who had moved in long after the kidnapping said not to do it, because who knew what unimaginable horrors might turn up.

Mom and Dad prevailed. They wanted one last try and they got it.

And they had been right.

Because there was one person who would recognize the picture, if she saw it.

Jennie herself.

As vividly as if she had fallen into the very cafeteria where it happened, Jodie imagined that moment of unwrapping a sandwich and picking up a milk carton. That moment in which Janie Johnson ceased to be a happy well-adjusted kid who wanted nothing more than a boyfriend and a driver's license. That moment in which she became a terrified wreck who eventually uncovered the truth.

Not that anybody, including Jennie, knew the truth.

Mrs. Spring had taken her five children shopping at the mall. It is not easy to shop with five children. An adult has but two hands, one if she carries packages. So the twins, staggering insecurely on bow legs, had had little red harnesses around their baby chests. Mrs. Spring kept their leashes wound around her right wrist, along with her purse handle. Stephen, six, and Jodie, five, were to hold each other's hands. Jennie, three and a half, clung to her mother's free left hand.

In the shoe store, Jennie had been a nuisance.

Jennie was jealous of the attention the others got. The others came in pairs and she did not. She was in the middle and it was not her favorite place. Jennie wanted not just the pretty new shoes, but also the matching patent-leather handbag. Jennie pranced around the shoe store, the handbag over her shoulder, demanding that her mother buy it and whining unmercifully when Mom said no.

The twins were difficult to fit. Their little toes curled under when the salesman tried to feel where their feet ended inside the shoes. He and Mom were kneeling on the floor, trying to coax the twins to stand up straight. The twins loved this game and kept falling over onto their diaper paddings and laughing themselves sick.

Stephen and Jodie were hugging their new shoes to their chests. There is just nothing like a new pair of shoes when you're little. Jodie loved the box as much as the shoes. She kept peeping inside the box to check on her lovely new-scented leather shoes, planning what she would do with the empty box when they got home. Stephen kept shifting his weight from one foot to another, saying, "Mom? Mom? Mom? I wanna wear my new ones. Mom? Mom? Mom? I wanna wear my new ones."

"Hush!" their mother kept saying, pressing down on a twin's toe.

It was not until they lined up at the cashier's desk that they noticed Jennie was not there.

Mom was furious. She yelled at Stephen and Jodie for not watching Jennie. Yanking the twins by their cords and the older ones by their linked hands, she marched out into the mall expecting to find Jennie window-shopping at the stuffed-toy shop, or watching the man who silk-screened your name on T-shirts while you waited.

But they did not find Jennie.

They never found Jennie.

Jennie was never seen again.

Twelve years later came the story none of them could have thought up.

It seemed that a Mr. and Mrs. Frank Javensen, of Connecticut, had had a daughter, Hannah. Many years earlier, teenage Hannah had joined a cult. This was a sort of religious group, which brainwashed its new, confused members—young, lonely, idealistic kids like Hannah. Cult members obeyed their leaders in every way, including where they sat, what they ate, whom they married. Cult members earned money for their leaders by selling anything from flowers to their own bodies. Once you joined, you never left. You were never given permission. You did not visit home, and you scorned your parents and everything that home and upbringing had once meant to you. Any word uttered by your leader was Truth. Any word uttered by your country, school, or family was Corruption.

Hannah, eighteen, was sucked in. She was so completely brainwashed she could speak only when spoken to and lost the ability to initiate anything. When the cult moved her to California she went. The Javensens hired private detectives to find her.

When they could not coax Hannah to come home, Mr. and Mrs. Javensen actually stole her back. Then they paid an expert to un-brainwash Hannah.

The plan failed. Hannah preferred the cult and back she went.

The years passed.

Hannah acquired a "mate" chosen by the leader and was married in a mass ceremony with hundreds of other couples. The Javensens knew there was no hope. They still wrote, but the letters were never answered, and they still phoned, but Hannah never came on the line.

And then one day, one ordinary suburban day, with no warning and no notice, Hannah came home. She just walked in, after all that time. She was not alone. She was with *her* daughter, a sweet little red-haired girl.

My daughter Janie, said Hannah. *I want her brought up in your world, not mine. I can't change my life, but I can save Janie from it.*

And back Hannah went, address unknown, needing whatever strange and sad things the cult had to offer her.

The Javensens, knowing the cult would claim and then whisk away this innocent grandchild as well, fled. Not only did they find another town, they even changed their unusual last name to a dull and unmemorable one. Frank and Miranda Javensen, whose daughter Hannah disappeared in the clutches of a cult, became Frank and Miranda Johnson, whose daughter Janie soon entered nursery school.

They didn't want little Janie to remember Hannah, nor pine for her, and certainly never to look for her, because a search would lead to the cult. So they taught Janie to call them Mommy and Daddy.

But Hannah had never had a child. It was a lie, one that Mr. and Mrs. Javensen had completely swallowed.

What had happened in that shopping center in New Jersey?

Hannah must have decided to leave the cult, fleeing California, stealing money to make the trip, and eventually stealing cars as well. Hannah would have been nearly at the end of her journey. Only a half day's drive from her home. Had she panicked? Had she been so desperate for company that even a three-year-old seemed attractive? Had she planned to ask for ransom money and then gotten scared? Had the cult told her to kidnap a baby? Had it been her idea, or could she actually have been assigned such an evil task?

What had motivated Hannah to pretend Jennie was hers? Had she given Jennie to the Javensens from fear of jail or of the cult? Or had Hannah become so demented from years without love that she was too confused to know herself? Had Hannah, kidnapped herself from her cult by her own parents, thought what she was doing was normal?

Unless Hannah was found, nobody would know those answers.

They had one answer to one question, at least: why hadn't the Javensens heard about the kidnapped Jennie Spring and realized it was this child?

They'd been running from the cult they were sure would snatch the baby back. That week there was no time for television, radio, or newspapers. And like any sensation, coverage of a missing child two states away ended, replaced by other sensations. By the time their lives reached normal (if name-changing and child-acquiring could ever be called normal), publicity on the Jennie Spring case had ended.

Why "Janie" instead of Jennie?

They could only suppose that when Jennie said her name, Hannah misunderstood.

Memories of her first three years faded. The little girl ceased to be Jennie Spring and became completely and wholly Janie Johnson, daughter of Frank and Miranda.

Then one day, the little girl looked down at a carton of milk, and all their intertwined lives were once more irrevocably changed.

Jodie took her mother's hand. She might have pressed a Scream button, the way Mom reacted.

Mom cried out, unable to bear Mr. Mollison asking all the questions. Asking, in her opinion, the wrong questions. "Did Hannah force you?" Mom sobbed.

Jodie began to cry in spite of her vows not to.

"No," said Jennie. Her voice broke. "I think I wanted to go. I think I was having fun."

Jodie's mother—and Jennie's—said softly, full of love, "I'm so glad. I saw you torn from limb to limb. I saw you beaten and bruised and left to die in some swamp. I saw you assaulted by horrible evil people. But you were okay. I'm so glad."

It was a cue, in Jodie's opinion. Jennie should have gotten up to embrace this real mother. The

Springs should have hugged all around. That would be the door to let them forgive and accept.

But Jennie held a pillow instead of a mother and looked away.

14

Mr. Mollison relaxed into the sofa cushions, as if he were the one who lived here. He slouched down till his feet stuck out into the room and began chatting comfortably and easily. He's trying to soften me up, thought Janie. She tried to resist him, though why she was resisting and whom she was protecting, she did not really know.

"Practically nobody," said Mr. Mollison, "is ever kidnapped by a stranger. In spite of the hype you see on television, there are probably no more than fifty children a year taken by strangers. Those victims are usually abducted for sexual purposes, and let go by their captors very quickly. In fact," said Mr. Mollison, rearranging the crystal candlesticks and the stacks of magazines on the coffee table, "these kids are usually home within a few hours. Most of the time the police aren't called until *after* the child is home and has told the parents what happened. Furthermore, most of those children are not babies and not toddlers. The children taken by strangers are young teens."

Janie was not in the mood for background material. She wanted Mr. Mollison to get to the point, get out of the house, and get out of her life.

It was her brothers and sister who listened. Stephen was astonished. "But then—who are all these missing children?"

"You have to define missing," said Mr. Mollison. "Missing includes late. Children who are late getting home. They misunderstood what time their parents told them to be home or they went somewhere else. Missing includes lost. A family can't find the kid and they live near a river, and maybe missing means drowned. Missing includes runaways. Children who purposely leave home, who don't want to be home. Missing includes children of divorce where one parent keeps them longer than he's allowed to by visitation rights. The other parent knows exactly where the child is and has probably talked to the kid on the phone. Missing is an inclusive word. Missing hardly ever means kidnapping."

"So you didn't know I was kidnapped," said Janie.

"Nobody knew anything. You were a three-year-old redhead in a polka-dotted dress who couldn't be found. Your family searched the mall. Security searched the mall. They made loudspeaker announcements. People didn't panic for a while," said Mr. Mollison. "Even when panic really set in, everybody figured you'd just wandered off. State troopers brought dogs to find your scent. Volunteer search teams held hands and inched through fields and woods for a half mile behind the mall. People waded through ditches and opened the trunks of abandoned cars."

Opened the trunks of abandoned cars? Janie's hair prickled. What if they had found her like that? A body thrown carelessly inside a rusting wreck, lying dead on mouse-chewed upholstery.

"Altogether," said her father in a queer collapsing voice, "there were six abandoned cars." He gave a funny strangled laugh. "Six," he repeated, and Janie knew that he was seeing each one of them. Mrs. Spring crushed herself against her husband's chest, protecting herself from the memories.

Six times, Janie thought, among the rats and the garbage, they poked and prodded to find a corpse. Mine.

For the first time she knew what they had been through.

Get up, Janie told herself. Go hug them both. These are your mother and father. You're the kid they thought would be found dead in the trunks of those six cars. Go to them!

But she did not. She looked down at her small sturdy hands and the shape of her fingernails. Her parents in Connecticut had completely different hands. Naturally.

"When the police began questioning people in the mall," said Mr. Mollison, "a waitress remembered a young woman with long blond hair and her little girl with bright red hair. She remembered them laughing together and leaving together. Holding hands."

"So you did know!" cried Janie. "You knew Hannah took me. What were you looking in cars for? Why did you make my parents go through that?"

"How could we know why the woman took

122

you?" said Mr. Mollison. "Maybe to kill you. Maybe she knew it was stupid and pushed you out of her car as she was driving away. At any rate, once the waitress identified your photograph, it ceased to be a missing-child case and became Abduction by a Stranger. Not one of the police involved in the case had ever before—or ever since, for that matter—handled that crime. Statistically, ninety-five percent of all police stations will not encounter child-abduction by strangers. Forget what you see on TV. It doesn't happen."

"Except to us," said Jodie.

There was a long period of quiet.

Janie could distinguish separate breathing, her mother taking air in little shudders, her father breathing hard through his nose, Stephen regulating his lungs like a machine, Jodie holding her breath, waiting.

"Except to you," agreed Mr. Mollison.

One of the policeman passed around two large boxes of Dunkin Donuts. Of course the good doughnuts ran out right away and the twins complained that there should be more chocolate-covered and fewer cream-filled. Mrs. Spring brought out perked coffee, a pitcher of milk, and plenty of mugs and glasses.

The Springs were great milk drinkers, going easily through a gallon a day and often more. Janie found herself with a glass of milk in her hand. She set it back down.

"I'm sorry, I forgot your allergy," said Mrs. Spring. She poured Janie a glass of apple juice instead. Janie found apple juice a dull excuse for a liquid but she took it.

"If you can't drink milk, what were you doing with a milk carton to start with?" asked one of the twins.

"I had a peanut butter sandwich," she said, "and you have to have milk with that."

Everybody nodded.

"Sarah-Charlotte was flirting with Pete. She wasn't looking. I had had my juice and I needed milk, so I took hers and drank it. And when I set it down . . ." Her mind had spun like a color wheel, each of the bright primary colors screaming: *No!— you have a father and a mother—a happy childhood —you were not kidnapped.*

As the facts spun like evil wool, weaving a truth Janie did not want, she had tried to think of nobody but Reeve.

This was fine by Sarah-Charlotte. They intensively studied the prom issue of *Seventeen* because Sarah-Charlotte was sure Janie'd be going to the senior prom with Reeve. "He hasn't asked me," Janie had objected.

"Boys never think farther ahead than the next meal. But you can't wear just anything, with that red hair. Let's pick a gown."

He's asked me, thought Janie, and I still have to pick a gown. But my life—where did my life go since then?

She stared through the doorway into the kitchen, where there were no eyes.

The knobs on the cabinets were white porcelain with tiny blue tulips. Dog-eared phone books curled over a rack by the wall phone. Over the sink a small window was lined with African violets. A frilly polka-dotted curtain was held back by red ribbons. On the wall was a plaque, painted by a child in an art class. A very out-of-proportion house with a stick family leaning out of the windows bore an address in willowy script.

114 Highview Avenue

"We never moved," said her father, following her gaze. "If the day came when you could get in touch, we had to be here."

Janie let go of the rest of her doughnut. Timidly, Mrs. Spring rested her hand on Janie's. Janie turned her hand over, curled her fingers one by one, and held her mother's hand. *These are my parents.* I know them by their suffering. I know by the price they paid.

I'm not sorry anymore that I saw the milk carton. I'm glad they don't have to worry. I'm glad they don't have to think about the trunks of abandoned cars. I'm glad to know them. But what about Mommy and Daddy? Are *they* going to be all right?

"You knew about Hannah before you came," she said to Mr. Mollison. "You've already found out most things. Why are you really here?"

"We need to find Hannah," said Mr. Mollison, casually, as if it hardly mattered, as if finding Hannah were just another boring activity.

"No, you don't," said Janie. "Everybody agreed we would let that go. We promised each other. Through Lizzie. It wasn't Hannah's fault, and even if it was, it wasn't my parents' fault, and even if it was, it doesn't count. We're not counting it. We agreed."

Mr. Mollison said gently, "Lizzie was wrong. She never studied criminal law, and she got her facts wrong."

Lizzie? Wrong? This had not happened in neighborhood history. Lizzie had never been one of Janie's favorite people. Lizzie had never been one of Reeve's either. His older sister was infuriating, pompous, and first in line even if she had to break other people's ankles to get there.

Janie could hardly wait to pick up the telephone. Reeve, she would say, it's me, and guess what—great news! Lizzie was wrong!

She and Reeve would party.

"I'm the victim," said Janie. "I was the one who was kidnapped and I refuse to prosecute the kidnapper. It's okay with me. I know it was wrong, and it hurt everybody, but Hannah is my parents' only daughter. You have to leave her alone. We agreed." She looked at Mr. and Mrs. Spring. "Didn't we?" she said.

A grief Janie could not identify crossed their faces: not grief for the pain of the last twelve years, but a grief for today. For Janie. The room expanded with things to come, pain waiting to attack.

"The law doesn't work that way, Jennie," said Mr. Mollison gently.

All this soft-spoken gentleness was getting on Janie's nerves. "Don't hurt my parents," said Janie, and weirdly, dizzily, *parents* meant all four adults who called themselves her mother and father.

"Nobody is going to hurt your parents," said Mr.

Mollison. "They aren't guilty of any crime. They really thought you were their granddaughter. In fact, we're grateful to Mr. and Mrs. Johnson, because they kept you safe and happy."

"Then why are you here?"

"After a crime has been committed," said Mr. Mollison, "and the police have been brought in, it stops being in your hands. The crime is still there, whether you consider it a crime or not. The person who committed the crime—in this case, Hannah Javensen—must be brought to trial. It doesn't matter that you and the Johnsons and the Springs agreed to forget it. The law does not forget. We will find Hannah and bring her to New Jersey to stand trial for kidnapping."

CHAPTER
15

"Two years ago," said Mr. Mollison, so slowly that the entire two years seemed to filter through the room, "Hannah Javensen was arrested in New York City. Her fingerprints are on file."

Two years ago! thought Jodie. When we were deciding whether to put Jennie's picture on the milk carton. When we were wondering if there was any point in dragging it up again.

Two years ago! thought Stephen. Then Hannah was local. She herself could have seen the milk carton. What if she had? Would she have remembered? Did Hannah ever realize what she did?

Two years ago! thought Janie Johnson. When I was happy and nothing had changed. When my parents were perfect and my bedroom was beautiful and my friends were wonderful and my street was home and—

She was exaggerating. Life is infrequently perfect. But her life had been closer than most. She had been surrounded by love as few are privileged to be.

Surrounded, thought Janie. My parents really

did surround me; I had my own private posse to protect me from the world. And now I have a second set surrounding me. I might as well be under house arrest for all they let me out of their sight.

She tried to imagine Hannah in New York City—equidistant from the two families—Springs to the south of her, Johnsons to the north of her. Had Hannah thought even once of what she had done? Or, in reverse, did she think of it all the time? Was guilt what brought her back East?

Janie had often gone into New York City with her parents. They loved the city. They loved its museums and restaurants and theaters. They loved to soak in the variety and the racket, the adrenaline and the chaos that was New York. Janie walked squarely between her mother and father. Surrounded, she thought.

What if we'd seen Hannah on the sidewalk? You cannot recognize a three-year-old twelve years later. Could you recognize a thirty-year-old twelve years later?

What if Mommy and Daddy and I were coming out of a restaurant, and on the other side of the street . . . alone and forlorn . . . was Hannah . . . watching people who were once her family being happy without her.

To be happy. Such a reasonable goal. Had Hannah stolen baby Jennie in order to find happiness? Or had she stolen a child to destroy somebody else's happiness? Lashing out, somehow, at a world she had chosen to leave behind?

As for two years ago, arrested in New York, had she tried to telephone her parents, only to find that no Javensen existed? Because Frank and Miranda Javensen had disappeared as completely as Jennie Spring. If Hannah had wanted help when she was arrested, she could not have gotten it from home.

Janie's mind felt like hair caught in a rubber band—twisted and ripping away.

"What did Hannah look like, anyway?" asked Jodie.

"There are pictures in the attic," said Janie. What terrible self-discipline! To put every single photograph of your own child into storage. What sort of failure had Frank and Miranda been, as parents, to create Hannah? What sort of failure had Hannah been, as a daughter, to hurt Frank and Miranda so much? "She had long, sleek white-blond hair. I always wanted hair that would lie flat on my back like that."

"Was she pretty?"

Janie considered. "In a limp sort of way. She was what Sarah-Charlotte calls Used Rag Doll." She was sorry she had said it. It was a form of betrayal to the Johnsons.

"Used Rag Doll," repeated Jodie. "I can see her perfectly. Nobody is ever best friends with that kind. They're always on the fringes. Doomed."

"Doomed," whispered Janie. She turned for the first time for solace from Mrs. Spring. "Do you think there is such a thing? I mean, do you think a person could really be destined for good or evil? Do you think Hannah was doomed?"

"No," said her mother. "That's what it is to be human. To make your own choices. Hannah was a weak teenager in bad times. Every turn in her life, she made the worst choice. But she was not doomed. She could have behaved differently. The rest of the world behaved differently." The tone of voice was so motherly that Janie was comforted even though it was not the mother she wanted.

"Was she religious?" asked Jodie. "Did she pray a lot and read the Bible for answers?"

Janie shook her head. "Daddy said that we weren't a religious family and she probably didn't know much about that. He said that in another time and age, Hannah would probably have become a nun and spent her life meditating and praying, but that nobody in our family knew anything about praying and nuns and the Bible, so it didn't come up."

The Springs exchanged looks. They were religious. They knew bunches about praying and nuns and the Bible. Janie felt a little cautious around the church part of their lives. She had been to Mass with them every week and found it a strange way to spend an hour.

"But she knew, didn't she?" said Stephen, excited. "Hannah knew that she needed to be religious. It was just a matter of finding a church."

"Yes, but she didn't find a church," said Janie. "Not a real one, anyway. She found a cult. Or actually, I guess the cult found her. A cult is a group that goes out and finds weak people like Hannah and preys on them, like hawks on mice. That's what my father says. They dig their talons in and never let go."

"Weak?" objected Jodie. "She sounds strong to me. Look what she did to us!"

"She didn't know she was doing that, though," said Janie. "She only knew she was holding hands with somebody." *Why am I defending Hannah? The woman ruined us, and I stick up for her.* "Hannah never wanted to play with dolls or ride a bike. When she was a teenager, she didn't care about boys or getting a tan or listening to the radio. She worried about goodness. About the nation. Whether it was behaving morally. She worried about right and wrong."

"I guess she liked wrong best," said Stephen.

"Stephen, try not to make things worse," said Mrs. Spring.

"Hannah worried about the unfairness of life. Why did her family have so much—money, love, housing, health, confidence, brains—and others so little? My mom could volunteer and come home happy because she'd done her share. But Hannah pointed out that poor people, or dumb or lost or sick people, didn't have a wonderful home to go back to, or a loving family, or a great wardrobe."

"She was right," said Jodie. "But everybody wonders about that. You drive by some incredible mansion and you think—how come we don't live there? You sit next to some incredible brain in class and you think—how come I'm not that smart? You try out for drama and your competition is this gorgeous princess and you think—how come she got born beautiful and I didn't?"

"You are beautiful, honey," said Mrs. Spring.

Here we are discussing Hannah's philosophy of life, thought Janie, *and the mother has to jump in and insist her kid is beautiful. I like Mrs. Spring.*

"Yes, but you see, Hannah never thought about anything else."

"*Anything?*" said Stephen.

"I know," said Janie. "I don't understand it either. You'd think at least once in a while she'd dance around, or kid around, or get on the phone, or be silly." Janie had never understood what kind of person Hannah must have been. Her father had said once that Hannah was a true child of the sixties. What could that decade have been like? From what Janie had seen, the rest of the sixties children had been going to Woodstock, and wearing granny glasses, and picketing for peace. So where did Hannah fit in?

"But what's a cult *for?*" said Brendan. "I still don't get it."

"It's for making money, mostly," said Mr. Spring. "You call yourself a priest of this cult you've just invented, and then you go out and find rich gullible kids who want somebody to take charge of them, and they give you all they have, and then you send them into the streets to beg for more."

It didn't sound to Janie like a great way to make an income, but it was word for word what her own father had said.

"Nobody would be that gullible," protested Stephen.

"I guess it's the first semester of college where they really get you," said Janie. "You're homesick and you're scared and you haven't made friends and classes are hard and you don't want to call home and admit it. You want somebody to help you, without having to ask, and the cult will. That's what my parents say. I don't get it either. I don't see why Hannah didn't just get sick of it and leave, but once you're in a cult, you don't leave. They own you. Even your brain."

"They wear costumes, depending on the cult," said Mr. Spring. "Yellow robes and shaved heads in some of them."

"No," said Janie. "I know she wasn't wearing a yellow robe. And if she ever shaved her head it was a long time ago before she took me, because she had very long hair." Janie had dipped so many times into the blurry, ancient memory of what must have been kidnapping that now she was not certain she remembered anything. The little details—a green counter—the napkins in a shiny metal box—were they really from a forgotten television episode?

Stephen watched emotions chase each other over Janie's face. He could almost see the kidnapping happening, in the folds and changes in her cheeks and around her eyes. It frightened him, the way she could vanish into the past like that and forget the people next to her, here in the present. He said loudly, "Why was Hannah arrested, Mr. Mollison?"

"Prostitution," said Mr. Mollison reluctantly.

Janie imagined Hannah on some dingy garbage-strewn corner in the dark of night, meeting a strange man, moving into the shadows of some horrible alley, and . . . She stopped herself. It was too awful. This was her parents' real daughter—Mommy and Daddy's little girl Hannah.

"How long was she in jail?" said Jodie.

"Overnight."

One night. Hannah's location had been known for one night. Two years ago.

"New York is a big city," said Mr. Mollison, "and two years is a long time. She could be anywhere now. Miami, Los Angeles, New York. She could be back on some rural commune in New Hampshire or Montana. She could be in San Diego or Bridgeport."

"Why didn't you arrest her for the kidnapping when you had her?" demanded Brendan.

"We didn't know she was the kidnapper until you people put the face on the milk carton and Jennie recognized herself. Hannah was long-lost."

A hooker, thought Janie. "Do my parents know?" she said to Mr. Mollison.

He looked at her with great pity. "Yes."

She hated Mr. Mollison then. "Why did you have to tell them?" she shouted. "Why should they have to deal with that?"

Mrs. Spring said quietly, "It isn't Mr. Mollison's fault that Hannah came to this, Jennie. Don't yell at Mr. Mollison."

More than anything she had ever resented, Janie Johnson resented being told by Mrs. Spring how to behave. She felt herself coming to a boil, deep down where it mattered. She wanted to smash her fist into all of them, to break their belongings into little pieces and swear viciously. She wanted to let go of every molecule of self-control and attack like a rabid animal. Through clenched teeth, she said, "I'm telephoning my mother and father."

Mr. Spring cut her off. "No, Jennie."

She could not believe it. What did he mean, *no*?

"What are you going to say to them?" he demanded. "Huh?"

He was mad at her. Not mad like a stranger who expected something else, but like a father who expected something more.

"Are you going to suggest that Mr. Mollison is lying? That Hannah is really a great kid, surfing somewhere in California?"

Neither of her Spring parents had yelled at her before. She was amazed how deeply it cut. And how right he was.

"You seem to think you're the only one suffering. Let me tell you something, young lady. Mr. and Mrs. Johnson are suffering ten times more than you are. Their real daughter Hannah is a criminal and a hooker and God knows what else. When they had you, they could pretend otherwise, but now they don't have you and they have to face the truth."

The volcano inside Janie died, replaced by tears so hot they scalded. *Oh, Mommy. Oh, Daddy. If I were home with you right now, I could make it better. It wouldn't hurt so much. I'd be your daughter and you could forget Hannah again!*

How could the happiness of her childhood have been built on such ugliness? The beautiful life she and her parents had led had been crushed like aluminum foil in the fist of a giant.

Hannah, weak and worthless, had been the giant.

Anybody can destroy the world, thought Janie. Even a Hannah.

Mr. Spring held out his arms to Janie, no longer

a blockade to keep her from the telephone, but a refuge for his child.

She wanted comfort so much. She wanted to be wrapped in arms that held her tightly. She wanted physical love from a father who cared how she behaved and where she lived.

She looked into his hug as if looking into the front door of a different house.

And stepped in, and let him hold her, and became his daughter.

16

Anything Janie knew of trials came from television, which cleaned up courtroom procedure and accomplished in an hour what in real life might take months. Television packed each episode with amusing attorneys, interesting witnesses, and at least one romance.

What would a real trial be like?

It would be in some dingy New Jersey courtroom. A squadron of police would haul a pathetic undernourished Used Rag Doll before a judge. Handcuffed. In prison clothes.

Her Connecticut parents would be there, watching their two girls: the adult doomed to the fringes and the teenager living somewhere else. How would they survive the trial, the assault of the media trailing after them, the pop psychologists analyzing where Miranda and Frank Johnson had gone wrong?

And her other parents would be there, too, because they would never let Janie be unescorted.

The court would call her Jennie Spring. She would testify. She would have to tell the truth, the whole truth, and nothing but the truth. Swear on a Bible. Answer the questions of an attorney who would look like Lizzie Shields: thin in the brutal way of women too busy and too ambitious to have time for lunch.

I went willingly. I didn't fight back. She didn't make me. It was fine with me. Those would be the answers to the questions.

Mommy and Daddy would endure exposure so complete Janie did not see how they would even leave the house, let alone come to New Jersey. They too would have to testify . . . *against their own daughter. Their* words would put Hannah in prison. Jennie Spring couldn't swear who took her when she was three . . . but Miranda and Frank could.

It was one thing for the Johnsons to believe that Hannah was safe (weird, but safe) in the enclosure of a cult. It was quite another to help put that same daughter in prison, with the human animals that would constitute the prison population.

It had never occurred to Janie that the police would go after Hannah whether or not she gave them permission. Janie was the victim. She had rights, didn't she? Hadn't her families suffered enough? Couldn't they just say—Quit that! Leave it alone!

No, it turned out. They could not.

Janie wanted to be left in peace to think about this horrible new development. But this was the real world. It included meals and homework, ball games, changing the sheets, finding a prom dress. There was no peace. There was not even five minutes alone, because this was the Spring household, and there were too many Springs for anybody ever to be alone.

Janie struggled with a history fill-in-the-blank homework sheet. The phone rang. She was closest to the kitchen wall phone, so she picked it up, although she rarely answered the Springs' phone.

"Hi. Sarah-Charlotte," said Sarah-Charlotte, who always began a conversation as if she were telephoning herself.

Janie had not talked with her former best friend since she left Connecticut. "Hi," she said, feeling cornered. Sarah-Charlotte would expect real conversation. Janie couldn't even think, never mind talk.

"I miss you," said Sarah-Charlotte excitedly, "but Reeve told me today about the prom! It is so neat! You'll be back here! We'll go together. You will absolutely never never never in a thousand million years guess who I'm going to the prom with, Janie." She waited for Janie to guess.

Janie was too disoriented to think of a single boy from the entire Connecticut high school. "Who?" she said at last.

"Devon!" shrieked Sarah-Charlotte. "Devon asked me out!"

Janie could not bring a Devon to mind. She could not bring anything to mind. She was not sure she even *had* a mind. "That's terrific, Sarah-Charlotte. Tell me about Devon."

Sarah-Charlotte told her about Devon.

Janie jumped herself up on the kitchen counter to sit with her feet dangling. She twirled the phone cord in her hand like a lasso.

On the kitchen table, the twins finished their homework and set up the Monopoly board. "Shove over, Jo," said Brendan. Jodie made an irritated face and moved her Japanese notebook exactly one inch. Jodie never heard anything when she was doing Japanese. She said it was so hard you had to put your ears and mouth and fingertips into it as well as your brain. That was enough of a clue for Janie; she'd stick with French.

"I stayed home from school today to think about what kind of prom gown I want," said Sarah-Charlotte. Sarah-Charlotte had had a habit of doing that kind of thing. She loved talk shows. If Oprah and Donahue looked sufficiently interesting, she pretended to have the flu. Sarah-Charlotte yearned to be part of a family that harbored some evil trait or scandalous past, so that she too could appear on national television and tell the world. But of course she had been born into a depressingly normal family whose biggest problem was forgetting the cents-off coupons when they went to the grocery.

Janie was not surprised when Sarah-Charlotte abandoned the prom-dress topic for a line-by-line discussion of the day's talk shows.

"You know, Janie, you could be a big hit on talk shows. Think of it!" said Sarah-Charlotte joyfully. "A panel of people who were once kidnapped and didn't even know it!"

I can hardly talk about it inside my own mind! How could I talk about it in front of a million strangers?

What made people do that? On television, they were asked questions nobody should ever be expected to answer. And yet they answered. They said things out loud that must have sliced through their hearts and souls, and damaged the people with whom they had to have supper that night and live with the rest of their lives.

And yet they answered.

Part of my problem, thought Janie, is that I don't want to answer. I don't want to talk to the Springs. I don't want to talk to the police. I don't want to talk to Sarah-Charlotte. I just want to go home, and be normal, and be what I was. I want to put the past in a drawer and never open it.

"Can't you just see the audience?" said Sarah-Charlotte, getting into it. "It would be dynamite." Sarah-Charlotte whooped. "You'd be famous."

Janie had always thought what fun it would be to be famous. Wrong. Because she was famous, in her way, at the new school. Strange eyes continually assessed her. Whenever kids sat down with her in the cafeteria or the library, she wondered why. Did they hope to be players in a game of What Happens Next?

Brendan dealt out Monopoly money.

It's all a game, thought Janie. We're just players on a board; eventually the game will end and we'll be dumped back into the darkness of the box.

Sarah-Charlotte imitated Oprah very well. She was playing Talk Show the way, when the girls were little, they once played House.

My best friend, Janie thought. I don't want to talk to her, I don't want to hear her voice, I don't want to waste time on this. "Listen, Sarah-Charlotte, I'm really sorry, but you know how it is in a house full of people." Sarah-Charlotte didn't, but Janie rushed on. "Jodie has to use the phone. I have to get off."

Jodie raised her eyebrows.

"Yes. Great talking to you. Say hi to Devon." Whoever he is. "Yes, I'll let you know what color my prom gown will be. Great. Great. Bye."

Jodie finished a vertical line of Japanese characters. "So," she said. "Do I get an explanation of this?"

Janie shrugged uncomfortably. "She was kind of annoying."

Jodie slammed her homework into a pile, her personal stamp of finishing up. "Caitlin and Nicole are annoying me right now, too."

Janie knew. She'd seen them. She was pretty sure it had something to do with her, but hated to ask. Why uncover yet another problem? "Sometimes," said Janie, "you wonder how you picked that person to be friends with anyway."

It softened Jodie to have Janie confide. Jodie leaned forward. "Are you going to double-date for the prom? What is Devon like?"

Janie had to giggle. It was a relief to know she still had the skill. "I never heard of him. Sarah-Charlotte told me I would never in a thousand million years guess who had asked her and she was right."

Mr. Spring bounded into the kitchen. "Hey! What's with the couch-potato posture?"

"Nobody's lying on the couch, Dad," said Brendan, buying a hotel. "This is a chairs and counter group."

"The first truly warm evening we've had this spring, you could be out in the yard practicing for baseball tryouts, we could be Rollerblading—and you're in here on the phone and playing board games. Everybody up. We're going skating together."

"Not me," said Mrs. Spring.

"Not me," yelled Stephen from the other room.

"Not us," said the twins.

"I'll go," said Janie.

The twins dropped their play money. Mrs. Spring sloshed her coffee over the edge of the mug. Stephen came in from the living room to look at her more closely. "We should have Sarah-Charlotte call more often," said Jodie.

Janie giggled right along with them. "Stop it. I just want some exercise."

Everybody went. How could they not, with Janie volunteering to participate for the first time ever?

Janie was getting better at this particular family hobby, though she still had to clutch somebody in order to stop. Three blocks away was a hill that was fine going up, but terrifying going down. "I'll hang on to you for the hill," Mr. Spring promised.

Janie nodded. They set off, Janie less steady than the rest, but keeping up, marginally. The twins vanished. Anything athletic brought out their competitive spirit. Stephen skated ahead, skated lazily back, circled Janie twice, and still got to the corner ahead of her.

"Show-off!" said Janie.

Stephen grinned. "Race you," he offered.

"No, but I'll accept a tow." She grabbed his belt. Now she need only balance and she sailed in Stephen's wake. It was great fun, the wind blowing through her hair, the success of skating without actually having to skate successfully.

This is why Hannah joined a cult, she thought. Hannah wanted a tow through life. And so do I. So do I! It's too hard, there are too many decisions, it hurts too much.

CHAPTER
17

Tomorrow was May 10. Her birthday. She would be sixteen.

Janie lay in bed, listening to Jodie snuffle, turn, mutter, and even creak like a door. She found it endearing now—this undefended person, who could not hear and could not see, innocently making her presence known.

It was incredibly important to turn sixteen. But nobody had said anything about Janie's birthday.

The Springs had an excuse—they didn't know. Frank and Miranda Johnson had made the birthday up. Hannah went back to the cult on May 10, leaving little Janie, and they honored it by making it Janie's birthday.

Her memory shot down a long parade of birthdays. They never had parties, with games and prizes and races. It was always a journey.

How vividly she remembered her ninth birthday, in which she and her parents, Sarah-Charlotte, and Adair O'Dell had gone to New York. Neither Sarah-Charlotte nor Adair had ever been to New York before, and so Janie had been the sophisticated hostess, showing off the Statue of Liberty and the elevators at the World Trade tower as if they were hers.

Her twelfth birthday, her father rented tents and took Janie and her seven best friends (in sixth grade you had multiple best friends) camping on Cape Cod. There had been sand dunes on one side of the campground and a miniature golf course complete with castles and pirates on the other. The water had been far too cold for swimming. Night was so cold they ended up two to a sleeping bag, giggling crazily till dawn.

Fourteenth birthday: just the three of them at Disney World. Janie had loved every minute of it, even standing in line.

Fifteenth—her last before the milk carton—her last before the world exploded—she and Mom flew to Washington. They'd done it all, from the Smithsonian to the Vietnam Memorial. This was when Janie decided to live in a city when she was grown up. None of this removed-from-the-world small-town stuff.

The Johnsons had never given presents on birthdays. Packages were for Christmas. Birthdays were for trips.

But they had done cakes. Fabulous sheet cakes special-ordered from the bakery. The year Janie was ten was the year of the Barbie doll; Janie and Sarah-Charlotte between them had every outfit that existed. The cake that year had featured Barbie skating on the icing. Mom had brought the cake into fourth grade, and the whole class dug in to have a bite of Ken or Barbie.

She had hoped to hear from Mommy and Daddy, wishing her happy birthday, but that was unfair. They knew all too well they had made up May 10. As for Reeve, who had been sending her cards wholesale, he'd never been invited on a birthday trip and probably didn't know her birthday. Boys, till recently, had been too icky to have around on important occasions.

I know your birthday, Reeve, she thought. February 28. You sneaked in eight minutes before leap year. I didn't send you a card this year either. I was busy being a whiny little creep with my new family.

Eventually it was one A.M., and then two. Love and sorrow kept her company through the long night.

If she crept out of the bedroom, down the thin hall, into the square kitchen . . . if she lifted the phone and dialed home, she was willing to bet her Connecticut mother was wide-awake, too.

Hannah, this is your fault, thought Janie. You did this to us. Where are you now, Hannah? You sick wrong bad mean horrible woman. I hope you're suffering. I hope life did something terrible to you. Because you did something terrible to all of us.

But I hope we never find you, Hannah. I hope that all the police and all the FBI in all the world cannot track you down.

Mommy and Daddy can't go through anything more. Do you understand that, out there in whatever hell you deserve?

Don't be found.

There's only one thing that you can do for the mother and father who gave birth to you.

Stay lost.

And then it was three A.M.

And finally four A.M.

Mrs. Spring often sang hymns to herself when she did housework. They were not familiar to Janie, who had not been brought up on religious music. She had learned a few of them from Mrs. Spring. "Balm in Gilead." "For the Beauty of the Earth." But the one Mrs. Spring sang most was "Amazing Grace."

"I once was lost," went the last lines, "but now am found. Was blind, but now I see."

At four in the morning, Janie found something. And could see.

She cried a little, but less than she would have expected. She felt certain, for the first time in so long. She also felt cruel.

When you do the right thing, thought Janie, it should be right all the way around. It shouldn't leave harsh edges. Just being right should be enough. But it isn't. I will be right, but I will be mean.

She was not sure what "grace" was, but she needed it, and the part of her that was a Spring prayed for it.

When Janie got up, after three hours of sleep, only Mrs. Spring was in the kitchen. "Good morning, Jennie," said her mother, breaking into a wide smile.

"Good morning."

Mrs. Spring boiled water for instant oatmeal and dealt bowls onto the table. She ripped the envelopes open, pouring Cinnamon Raisin in one, Apple Nut in another.

At home, Mommy would be making French toast. They always had French toast and bacon and eggs on Saturdays. That was why Reeve had breakfast with them. His own mother was sick of breakfast, having announced years ago that anybody who still wanted breakfast knew where the cereal boxes were.

Janie stirred her oatmeal until it thickened and became semi-real. She reviewed her four A.M. decision and it was still correct and still right . . . and still cruel.

I am sixteen—even if the calendar says I'm not.

I am Janie Johnson—even if the birth certificate says I'm Jennie Spring.

I am the daughter of Miranda Johnson—even if this nice woman is really my mother.

The world settled like a blanket on a bed, gently, filling in the dips and wrinkles. I am going to be like Hannah before me, thought Janie, crushing them in my fist as if they were aluminum foil. "Mom?"

Mrs. Spring beamed, so infrequently did she hear that word from this member of the family. "Yes, honey?"

Janie's heart pounded. Her hand on the stainless-steel spoon became sweaty. Her head ached. Her clothes felt loose. Her tongue was thick. "Mom, I want to go home. For good. I'm sixteen today. Even

150

if that birthday is not true for you, it's true for me. I tried. Stephen and Jodie are right, I didn't try as hard as I could have, but I tried some. I'm sorry. I truly am. I'm getting to like all of you very much. But my mother and father need me. I love my parents, and they're not you, and it's time to go home."

All her life she would carry with her the expression on this woman's face. The moment in which Janie took away hope and light. The sagging of Mrs. Spring's cheeks. The slow, stunned closing of her eyes.

This is my mother, thought Janie, and look what I'm doing to her.

Her real mother's hands trembled. She had trouble finding the chair and she sat down heavily, too heavily, as if into a grave. Emotional pain was so *physical.* You could never get away from your body.

"No," whispered Mrs. Spring.

Look what I am doing to this woman who did not ask for it. She did not ask for it from Hannah and she did not ask for it from me. How could the world dish this out to her? thought Janie. But the world isn't. I am.

She nearly said she was sorry, nearly said she didn't mean it, she'd try harder, stick it out. But the words did not come. Her heart was elsewhere.

Or perhaps, thought Janie, I have no heart.

"You know the words in your hymn, 'Amazing Grace'? *I once was lost, but now am found. Was blind, but now I see."* Janie could hardly go on. "I see now which is my real family. The people who brought me up. The people who need me most."

Janie's voice broke when she used it again. But that did not stop her from using it again. "School is out in six weeks," said Janie, "and I want to go back home then."

CHAPTER

18

Jodie and Stephen were stunned.

"I thought we were doing so well," whispered Jodie. *It's my fault,* she thought. I pushed too much. I demanded too much.

Jodie's daydreams—the old ones when she wondered what a sister would be like—came back like a movie rented for the VCR. The daydreams had no more to do with reality than Hollywood. In daydreams, sisters laughed about boys, shared clothes, told stories into the night, were each other's best friend.

She has a best friend, thought Jodie. Sarah-Charlotte. If that isn't the most show-offy pretentious name I ever heard in my life. And a boyfriend. *Reeve.* Please. It's not even a name. It's just a syllable.

"I hate her," said Jodie.

The family had sent Jennie to Uncle Paul's for dinner so they could talk without her there. Now they held hands around the table, not to bless the meal, but once more for a missing child.

Jodie's hand was held by Brendan on one side

153

and Brian on the other. The twins were just not very interested. They were consumed by their own lives. Jennie had not really entered into their thinking.

Jodie decided if you put your mind to it, you could hate everybody on earth for something. She already hated Jennie. She was perfectly willing to hate Brendan and Brian because they weren't upset at what this was doing to the family. She certainly hated Mr. and Mrs. Johnson. If she ever met Sarah-Charlotte, she would be sure to hate her, too. Reeve —well, Reeve was too cute to hate.

"I refuse to share the same bedroom with Jennie for six more weeks," said Jodie. "I might put a knife through her. Make her sleep on the couch."

"Just let her go back to Connecticut now," said Stephen. "What difference is six weeks of school?"

"Let her walk," said Jodie. "She doesn't even deserve a ride."

"She's your sister," said their father with terrible sadness, "and my daughter. And we're going to be nice to her up to the last minute no matter how we feel inside. I don't care how much discipline it takes. Whatever memories of this family she carries away the second time around, they're not going to be ugly or frightening."

Instead of dipping into his chocolate pudding with the spoon he held in his right hand, he bent it, and went on bending it until it was entirely round. The twins were awestruck.

"Wow, Dad," said Brian. "Do it with mine."

Dad did it with Brian's. He held up the now circular spoon. "That," he said, "is what I would like to do with Hannah's neck."

Everybody giggled hysterically.

"What would you really do to Hannah if you found her, Dad?" said Jodie.

"I'd like to beat her to a pulp," said their father gloomily, "but I suppose in reality, if we found Hannah she'd be a pathetic middle-aged mental case."

"It's nicer thinking of her as a teenager," said Jodie. "Blond and dishwatery and Used Rag Doll. I'd tie her to the railroad tracks and watch the next train cut her in pieces."

Everybody laughed again.

"This is sick," said Mom. "Now we're not going to talk like this again."

"Why not?" said Stephen. "I think this is great. Look what Hannah did to us! Why can't we cut her in pieces? In the Middle Ages they quartered people."

"Quartered people?" said Brendan. "What does that mean?"

Stephen drew a stick figure on his paper napkin, tilted his chair back from the table to reach the utensil drawer, and pulled out the kitchen scissors. Carefully he cut the napkin into fourths, right through the stick figure's waist. "They chopped 'em into four pieces back then," said Stephen with considerable satisfaction.

"Eeeuuuhhhh! Did we do that in America, too?"

"There were no Middle Ages in America, dumb-o," said his sister. "White people hadn't gotten here yet. Only Europe had Middle Ages."

"I hope they were alive when they got quartered," said Stephen. "Can't you just picture old

Hannah tied by the ankles and wrists while we take a long rusty dull saw, and divide her into quarters?"

"Yes," said their father. "I can picture it and I like it."

"Jonathan," said their mother warningly.

"Okay, okay, I'd let the police come along and restrain me," said Mr. Spring. "But I'd get in at least one good kick in the shins."

"Have we heard anything from Mr. Mollison?" Jodie asked her parents. "What kind of progress are they making on finding Hannah?"

"None," said her mother. "They never will. Most of those cults disbanded or threw their older members out on the streets. Discarded them like waste paper. Hannah won't have left a trail."

"Then why did the police make such a big deal of interrogating Jennie and opening the case up again?" cried Jodie. "Jennie going home is the police's fault." It had to be somebody's fault. Preferably the fault of somebody within reach so she could hurt them back.

"Maybe for publicity," said her mother. "Or curiosity. Or perhaps the law bound them. I think they were just fascinated and wanted to be part of the action again. Except there turned out to be no action on the Hannah front. Only on the family-collapse front. The police aren't keeping track of that. It isn't criminal. It's just tragic."

"I do not wish to talk about Hannah again," said Dad. "Not now, not ever, not on this earth, not in hell."

Brian grinned. "Sounds pretty final." Brian began eating with his now-circular spoon. Brendan,

156

envious, handed his spoon to Dad to circularize. Dad bent it willingly.

Dad's thinking of Hannah, Jodie thought, but the twins are thinking only of spoons. Jennie's fading for them before she's gone. "Is Jennie going to stay till school's out?"

Mom was crying, the kind Jodie hated: tears sliding out on their own, from a bottomless pit of pain. Jodie wanted to drive back and forth over Jennie's body in a truck with nail-studded tires. "Mom? Don't you think Hannah must have known what she was doing?"

Her mother didn't answer.

"The Johnsons and Jennie want to believe that Hannah was a sweet lost soul. A dear girl of a spiritual nature led astray by stronger minds. And she just happened to hold hands with the first friendly person she met, who just happened to be a three-year-old. I don't believe that."

Jodie's mother shrugged. She took the photograph of little Jennie, the one they had given the newspapers twelve years ago and the one they had put on the milk carton last year. "I'm losing her again. My baby girl. I'm losing her twice."

"I think," said Jodie, "Hannah knew perfectly well she was kidnapping Jennie. If Hannah had really been a mental case, she wouldn't have pretended Jennie was her own daughter. She wouldn't have pretended it was their granddaughter. I don't think Hannah was afraid of the cult. I think she was afraid of the police. Hannah ran away so her parents would be the ones who would get in trouble."

"What difference does it make?" said her

mother. "We're not going to have Jennie now, and the only improvement is that I don't have to worry whether she's safe or well or scared." Mrs. Spring laughed in despair. "I only have to worry that she doesn't want me, doesn't love me, and needs to finish growing up with somebody else."

Jodie, Stephen, and Dad watched the silent slide of tears.

Finally Dad said, "Stephen, I think you're right. It would kill us to keep pretending. The only reason to stay is school, and she might just as well finish school up there."

Jodie's rage was so great it was a pit bull and had her by the throat.

"You are scum," said Jodie in the dark, in the quiet, of their bedroom. She didn't care what the parental instructions were. Mom and Dad didn't have to undress in the same room with Jennie. They didn't have to fall asleep listening to rotten worthless Jennie breathe.

"I know that," said her sister. "I haven't been a good daughter, and I haven't been a good sister. I just want to go home. What happened, happened. That's that. I'm not going to pretend anymore."

"There wasn't any pretending!" cried Jodie. "You really and truly are my sister! You really and truly are Mom and Dad's daughter. That happened, too!"

The silence lasted. Jodie hoped that Jennie would have cardiac arrest from shame and badness.

"I don't know if there is a right thing morally,"

said Jennie at last. "Every choice in this is second best. So I picked a second best. I'm going home."

Jodie lay flat on her bed, staring up at the ceiling, keeping her hands stiff at her sides. She felt laid out, like a corpse. "We weren't good enough for you, were we?" she said.

"You are good! This is a very good family! I'm the one who's not good."

"Why can't you think of Mom? Think what this is doing to her! You are leaving her twice, and each time because it's more fun someplace else!" Jodie hung on to her sheets to keep from leaping across the room and shaking Jennie by the throat. "You're spoiled. You were a spoiled-brat three-year-old, and now you're a spoiled-brat teenager! You're going because the Johnsons have a better house! You get your own bathroom. That's what this comes down to. You're sick of waiting in line for the shower!"

The pause was very long.

"I hope not," said Jennie, her voice quavering. "I hope I'm a better person than that." She sounded three years old, in need of a hand to hold.

Jodie got out of bed, took the single step required to cross the little lane of rug between them, and lay down next to Jennie on top of the covers. "I thought we were doing so well," said Jodie. "I thought you were getting happy." Two thin blankets lay between them. There would always be something between them. "Were you acting?" said Jodie.

Jennie lay still.

"I want you to know something," said Jodie. Her throat swelled hideously. "We weren't acting. We were happy. We were glad to have you home."

159

Jodie sat cross-legged on her bed as Janie emptied the bureau drawers: the half of the room Jodie had so optimistically, so childishly, prepared.

Jennie had too much for her three suitcases. Now she was filling brown-paper grocery bags. Very neatly she folded sweaters to the exact dimensions of the bag and very neatly lowered them on top of each other.

"We're not going to have a life as neat as that," said Jodie, "after you've gone. Do you think we'll just lie here, neatly stacked? Color coordinated, like shirts on a shelf? Do you think you've been fair? Do you think you've been kind?"

Janie could not meet her sister's eyes and stared out the window instead. It was a warm day— wild and wonderfully windy. The sun was gold and the sky was cloudless and all the earth felt like a gift. Here we are! the world was saying. Just what we used to be! Loving, flawless, and good. Come home! We're waiting!

When she had telephoned home to tell her Johnson parents she had permission to come back for good, even those parents said what Jodie said. *We have to be fair: we have to do the right thing by your birth family, we have to—*

But her Connecticut mother paused. "Forget fair," whispered Mommy. "Come home."

No matter what Janie chose, she could be fair only to half the people involved.

She thought of all divorcing parents whose children were forced to decide whether to live with Daddy or to live with Mommy. Tons of kids had to make this decision. Which parent to go to? Which parent to slap in the face? Nobody deserves a slap, thought Janie. Unless it's Hannah.

"This is the best I can do," she said to her sister.

Jodie Spring shook her head once. "You didn't do your best. Not by us, anyway."

It was true, so Janie said nothing.

She lined up the suitcases, the cardboard boxes and paper bags by the bedroom door. Mr. Spring had said good-bye to her early that morning, when he took the twins to their baseball game. He looked a hundred years old. He had put his arms around her and she had wept but he had not. He said sadly, "We love you, sweetie. Take care of yourself."

There were few words for a man whose child wanted her other father.

The twins unemotionally waved good-bye. She had hardly made a dent in their existence, nor they in hers.

Mrs. Spring was driving her to Connecticut. Janie would not pick out her prom gown with Jodie and Mrs. Spring after all. She would not see a single baseball game of the twins' and she would never play Nintendo with a brother and sister again. She was going home to finish the school year where Adair and Pete and Katrina and Sarah-Charlotte would have lunch with her and Mr. Brylowe was her English teacher and Reeve would drive her each way in his Jeep.

Janie could hardly wait to see the huge blue turnpike signs with their immense white letters:

> **WELCOME TO NEW ENGLAND**
>
> **CONNECTICUT AND POINTS NORTH**

When she crossed the state line, it would be solid; it would really be over, she'd wake from the nightmare at last.

She could not look at her New Jersey mother, who had to stay in the nightmare.

Stephen silently loaded Janie's belongings into the car. Janie was actually slightly surprised that Stephen had not killed her. He'd wanted to. "You," Stephen had said, "deserve to be dead." Now he was arranging her belongings with great care, so nothing would tip or rattle. As if it mattered.

In a dreadful circle of events, it was now Mrs. Spring who would bring her daughter to Miranda Johnson, just as Hannah had done twelve years ago. It was Mrs. Spring who would place her baby girl's hand in the hand of the woman who would be her mother from now on.

She loves me enough to give me up, thought

Janie Johnson, but I don't love her enough to give up anything.

Jodie, Stephen, Mrs. Spring, and Janie stood on the driveway. Nobody touched. Stephen extended his hand and it took Janie a moment to realize he meant her to shake it. This is my brother, she thought. Don't sisters and brothers hug when they say good-bye? *Stephen's been a brother, but I haven't been a sister.*

She shook his hand.

"Tell your mother," said Stephen, "thank you for inviting us up for the weekend." Janie could not imagine what it had cost him to refer to Mrs. Johnson as Janie's mother. "Brendan and Brian aren't going to come, but Jodie and I will. So we'll see you in a month."

Such a gentleman. Janie looked sideways at him, wondering.

"Don't worry," he said. "I won't poison the sandwiches." His control slipped and vanished. "It's you Johnsons who do that kind of thing," he spat out. "Hannah, she thinks nothing of stealing cars and babies. And Janie, she thinks nothing of destroying families and damaging—"

"Enough, Stephen," said Mrs. Spring.

Stephen stopped.

For his mother's sake, thought Janie. He loves her enough to give her what she needs. And I don't.

Jodie touched Janie's shoulder. It was hard for her, and the closest she could come to an embrace. Jodie shrugged, and bit her lip, and stepped back. Janie wanted to fling her arms around Jodie, tell her that she was a wonderful person—

But instead she gave Jodie a tight and trembling smile, and quickly climbed into the front seat. Mrs. Spring sat behind the wheel. They backed out of the driveway. Janie waved. Neither Jodie nor Stephen waved back.

The car pulled away. The red house disappeared. They left Highview Avenue, and in a little while they were on the interstate, heading north.

Once they commented on traffic, noting a close call by a poor driver. They did not discuss their mission. In northern New Jersey, Mrs. Spring pulled into a service area to get a cup of coffee. They left the car and went into the restaurant. Janie got a Pepsi. At the end of the cafeteria line, Mrs. Spring paid for both drinks. It was a transaction that absorbed her deeply. Tears welled up in her eyes as she accepted her change, and Janie thought: this is the last thing she will ever do for this daughter.

"I want you to know I'm sorry," said Janie.

They walked stiffly, each trying not to cry.

"I don't know why I went with Hannah," said Janie. "I want you to know I'm sorry I did it. I know that Hannah didn't make me. I know she didn't use force. Jodie and Stephen are absolutely right. You can blame me for everything."

Mrs. Spring seemed unaware of the stink of exhausts and the roar of traffic. She looked up into that same lovely windy blue sky they had left an hour ago and blinked hard. "No. It's my fault, sweetheart. Don't take this on your shoulders."

"Your fault?"

"You were the middle child. A pair of kids above you and a pair of kids below you. The twins took up

164

tremendous time and attention. They were in diapers, they were yellers and screamers, they were kickers and fighters. Jodie and Stephen could do things in a pair. Even though in some ways they were antagonists, they were inseparable. And there you were in the middle." Janie and Mrs. Spring went down the wide cement steps from the restaurant into the parking lot. Janie tried to remember where they had parked the car. "I didn't have quite enough time," said Mrs. Spring. "I tried, but . . . the twins . . . in the shoe store that day . . . you stormed off. You were only three but you had a mind of your own. I'm sorry, sweetheart, that . . . *oh, God!* I'm sorry!"

Now Janie was weeping. "No! From the minute I saw my face on the milk carton, I knew I was the one who had been bad. Because my parents couldn't have been."

"You were three, Jennie. Three-year-olds aren't bad. The only person to blame is Hannah, and Hannah is out of reach. There's no point in laying blame."

They reached the car. Set their drinks on the hood while they fumbled for the locks. Hesitantly, Mrs. Spring ran her fingers over Janie's face. Janie flung her arms around Mrs. Spring in a hug so tight it hurt her own muscles. Their tears mixed when they touched cheeks.

"Good-bye, honey," said her real mother. Her voice was barely audible. Her last three words were more breath than speech. *"I love you."*

CHAPTER

20

$\mathbf{S}$tephen helped Jodie move the second bed out. Jodie could not stand to look at it, the bed her sister was supposed to be in. They hammered apart the railings and dismantled the headboard and footboard. Stephen yanked the cord to the disappearing attic stairs and with considerable difficulty hoisted each piece into the low-ceilinged heat trap. "She left her Jennie things," said Jodie.

"Her what?"

"Her mug, her book bag, her headband, her key ring—all the stuff Mom and I bought for her that say J E N N I E."

"You want to smash them or pack them?" said Stephen seriously.

The violence had gone out of her. Jodie could think only of her mother, taking that terrible drive, meeting the Johnsons, having to leave and drive home alone. Would she make it? Could she manage that return trip? Why hadn't they gotten that lawyer again, or else Reeve?

But Mom had insisted. "I have to," Mom had

said, refusing to explain. "I have to take Janie there myself."

"Janie?" Jodie had repeated.

"That's who she is. She stopped being Jennie when she was three and a half."

Jodie looked at the J E N N I E things. "We'll take them to the Salvation Army. We're not going to have a Jennie collection in the attic, the way the Johnsons saved Hannah. It's too sick."

"It's Hannah's fault," said Stephen. His eyes were bright with rage and hatred.

Brother and sister thought of the suffering and fear and endless burden of worry their mother and father had borne. Every minute and every hour and most of all, every night, spent wondering: *Is she all right? Is she hurt? Is she safe? Is she dead? Is she afraid?*

They thought of their mother's sleepless excitement in December and January, when she knew she was getting her daughter back; their father's desperate eagerness to hold his baby girl again.

They thought of Janie Johnson: somebody else entirely, who chose to go back to another set of parents.

"I'm going to get Hannah for this," said Jodie, filled by an ancient primitive ache. Revenge sounded hot and rewarding.

Her brother's eyes narrowed while he considered it.

"I want to hurt her back," said Jodie. "The police aren't really looking. It's not a priority for them. They have murders happening this afternoon. Why would they bother with a twelve-year-old kidnap-ping where the kid is safely home again?"

It was true. After the little flurry of activity, which in Mom's opinion was just bald curiosity—greedy peeking into private lives—the investigation had dried up.

"The FBI won't do anything unless some local police force turns her up," said Jodie. "We can look instead. Hannah was in New York two years ago. I bet she's still there. I bet we can find her."

"But there are millions of people in New York," said Stephen. "What are the odds of us finding the one person we want?"

"What were the odds of Hannah Javensen find-ing a three-year-old from *our* family? If she could do it, we can do it."

New Jersey had excellent public transpor-tation into Manhattan. Commuter trains and buses were frequent and easy to get. The trains went straight to Penn Station and the buses went straight to the Port Authority. Prime locations for lost souls.

Stephen and Jodie were two of the most super-vised teenagers in America. Getting into New York without parental permission was going to be a trick and a half. Could they possibly go with parental permission and fake it? Stephen cast his mind around for a good New York-visit excuse. Not once had the Spring children been allowed to go into the city without their parents. Stephen had even been refused permission to go on a school field trip to the Metropolitan Museum of Art because his mother was afraid a kidnapper would be lurking behind the pillars in the Egyptian Room.

"Uncle Paul and Aunt Luellen talked Mom and Dad into taking a rest," he said slowly to his sister. "They're going to Williamsburg in a couple of weeks. The twins are staying with the McKennas."

"We have to stay with Uncle Paul and Aunt Luellen," Jodie reminded him.

"We could finesse them." Stephen nodded. He lost himself in the daydream of getting into New York City without a chaperone. Dumping adults. Being a normal seventeen-year-old for once in his life! Everybody he knew could go into the city with their friends.

"How will we start?" said Jodie, meaning Hannah, not escaping from Uncle Paul and Aunt Luellen.

"We know a few things about her. We know she's used to being in a group and taking orders. So she'd find some way to duplicate that. We know she's used to having things provided for her, like meals. We know—"

"She'd use a soup kitchen!" said Jodie. "She doesn't know how to earn a living. Either the cult provides it for her or she has to beg or steal." Or hook. "How many soup kitchens do you think New York has?"

"There can't be that many."

"How would we find out where they are?"

They thought about it. "Janie found out about her kidnapping by looking it up in *The New York Times*," said Jodie. "So we can look up soup kitchens there. We'll put together a list."

"Dad would kill us," said Stephen. "Soup kitchens aren't going to be in the best sections of town."

"But he won't know. And we'll be safe because we'll be together, and it's May, so it'll stay light a long time. We can get into the city really early, and hit the soup kitchens at breakfast, lunch, and supper."

"We'll have to get home by dark," said Stephen. "Uncle Paul and Aunt Luellen aren't going to fall for any excuse that keeps us away after dark."

"That'll be easy. Soup kitchens serve supper early."

"How do you know?"

"I bet a dollar the homeless don't eat fashionably late," said Jodie.

They had the photograph of Hannah that the FBI had requested from Mr. and Mrs. Johnson. Hannah the limp but pretty teenager, with the straight, glossy white-blond hair. They could show the photograph around.

The adult part of Stephen's seventeen years knew the odds. Million to one that they could find Hannah Javensen. But the raging part of Stephen, the part he had carried through life, biting down on it, fighting it, trying to subdue it—that part rejoiced. He would have something to do. He could hit back. He could at least try.

They could not get revenge through hurting Janie. She really was their sister, and they really had not been acting. They really had been glad to have her home.

170

And they could not hurt the Johnsons, because Janie was back with them.

But they could hurt Hannah. Draw and quarter her. Circle her throat. Tighten their grip.

"Yes," said Stephen. "Let's get her."

CHAPTER
21

The tennis lesson was the flirtiest, silliest afternoon Janie had ever spent. She spun home. The kiss Reeve gave was soft and quick, like a brush of silk, or a promise. She and Reeve had been able to pick up exactly where they left off, as if there had been no nightmares, no second families, no Hannah, no school in New Jersey.

But at home—oh, at home, it was different.

They could not pick up where they had left off. She had never dreamed, in all her homesickness, that what she dreamed of would have changed so immensely.

Her mother's elegance and soul were frayed.

Her father's silver hair and courage had thinned.

They were old, these parents of hers, and they were different. Now they were afraid.

Life had hit them too many times, and too hard.

When she had said to herself *they need me*, she had not dreamed how much. In fact, Janie was a month away from her sixteenth birthday, and was still a child. She had expected to be held and coddled and warmed. Instead, she had to do the holding, and coddling, and warming.

But she had never loved them so much.

Don't be afraid, she thought. It will be all right. I will *make* it be all right. We've gotten past everything else and we're going to get past this.

It actually was like wedding vows. For Janie, they were parent vows. For better or for worse. For richer or for poorer. In sickness and in health. These are the parents I have chosen.

If I had done this in New Jersey, Janie thought . . .

But she had not. For better or for worse, she had not tried this hard in New Jersey.

"Remember how we used to picnic at the beach?" said Janie.

They'd had a favorite spot, a long long walk from the parking lots, through the high grasses and up on a bluff of wind-worn boulders. There they brought a hamper full of wonderful food and sat watching the sailboats on the horizon and the swimmers down below.

She was rewarded with their smiles. Scared smiles, afraid that Janie would go again and the nightmare would endlessly recycle.

"Remember the football cake I made?" said her mother.

Cake decorating had turned out to be her mother's one and only artsy-craftsy skill. But the way Janie remembered it, the football cake had been taken to a college game, not a beach picnic.

Memory had turned on Janie so many times that she had lost faith in it. Had the hampers had really been full of wonderful food, or had they just brought sacks of peanut butter sandwiches? Where had they had that football cake?

But details didn't matter. What mattered was the warmth in the memory, and the warmth came from being a family, from the constancy of family love. "Let's make a sheet cake tonight and decorate it, Mom."

Her mother beamed. "I haven't decorated a cake since—" The once-confident voice faded and the once-certain eyes blinked nervously.

"Since I left," said Janie. "Well, now I'm home. What'll we put on the cake? Do we have chocolate shots and silver balls?"

Her mother looked around, as if trying to identify what those might be.

"I think we keep cake-decorating stuff in the cupboard next to the canned goods," said Janie, and she was right. She waved the sparkles like prizes. She convinced her mother to put on an apron and get out the white-cake recipe. She convinced her father to find the measuring cups and plug in the mixer.

Where had Janie heard this cajoling voice she was using? Where had she seen somebody bend over lovingly in just this way? In whom had she seen this tilt of the head, this coaxing into cheery action?

In Mrs. Spring. Her biological mother.

Her hair prickled.

I really am Jennie Spring.

She had to turn away from the Johnsons, to

174

hide the sudden chill that went from her palms to her shoulder blades.

You can't be both, she thought. You can't be Jennie Spring as well as Janie Johnson. You've chosen Janie.

Now be Janie.

Be the best Janie there is, and never, never, never look back.

"Dear Janie," Stephen's mother wrote. Her tears spattered on the paper, leaving little raised bubbles for Janie to see.

Stephen hoped Janie cried, too.

But he didn't know if Janie worried about right and wrong the way Hannah had. He didn't even really know what was right and wrong in this situation. He only knew that every move hurt. His mother had arthritis of the heart. She was aching in every joint of the soul.

"Mrs. Johnson," said Stephen, "never wrote to Hannah again."

"What are you talking about?" said Dad. Dad growled whenever the name Johnson came up. His beard actually bristled, like a cat's back.

"When Hannah left the baby with them," said Stephen, "when they changed their name, and moved, to keep the cult from following, they never wrote to their daughter again. They never wrote on her birthday and they never wrote on Christmas. *They never wrote.*"

"I doubt if Hannah minded," said Mom.

"Don't write to Janie," said Stephen.

"I have to. I can't let go. I can't see how Frank

and Miranda Johnson let go of Hannah." His mother labored on, penning pointless sentences that Janie would not want to read, about the twins playing baseball and Stephen finding a summer job.

Stephen thought of the trip to New York. We are going to get Hannah. She is going to pay.

Janie lay in the bedroom for which she had so longed, actually missing the presence of Jodie. She listened for the sounds of Jodie breathing and turning, Jodie who was so noisy and demanding even in sleep.

Jodie would understand what she was going through, trying to climb back into her old life. Jodie would cringe for her. Jodie would be nice, in her prickly way. After Jodie finished telling her off, Jodie would hug. *We do love you,* she would say.

Janie had left the letter from Mrs. Spring untouched on her dresser. The handwriting on the return address bore an unexpected resemblance to her own. Now, slowly, she slid her finger under the flap and slowly drew the letter out of the envelope.

Dear Janie,

I need to write and hope my letters will not be a nuisance or a burden. We miss you but we respect your decision.

The twins are playing baseball. There are two other sets of twins on their team!

Stephen has his first job. He is a checker at Super Stop & Shop on Sundays. He is very proud of his paycheck.

Jodie and Nicole dyed their hair blond. I was furious, but your father just laughed.

Your father wants us to look for a bigger house now that we know where you are. So we're house-hunting. I wish we were planning a bedroom for you, too. You know that you can always visit. Al-ways.

Please write and tell me how your life is going.
     With love,
      your New Jersey mother.

Oh Mom! she thought, swamped in pain. Fire burned where her heart should be. Her tears spattered the paper on which other tears had fallen.

Hannah, what you have done to us!

Don't do any more, Hannah.

Stay lost.

CHAPTER
22

New York City at its finest.

The sun was yellow, the sky was clear, and a trillion windows in thousands of buildings glittered like diamonds.

The streets were swept, Penn Station was clean, and the homeless, if there were any homeless, had gotten up off their sidewalks and joined the crowds. Friday of Memorial Day weekend, and it seemed that half America had decided to memorialize in Manhattan.

Tourists from Europe and Japan and Long Island packed the intersections. Families holding children's hands walked abreast. A school group wore matching T-shirts and stood in a double line, snaking after their teachers. Messengers were on bikes, kids were on roller blades, cops on horses. Blizzards of paper handouts were stuck in their faces. (They could get film developed readily in New York.) Foreign languages surrounded them briefly and vanished like a weak radio transmission. There were enough pigeons to supply the cities of the world. People who worked in midtown poured from their offices to eat lunch outside, smile at the wonderful weather, and rejoice that they were part of the Big Apple.

It was not what Jodie had had in mind.

She had expected dreary desolation. Wasted leftovers of humanity staggering through garbage-filled gutters. She had expected the bathroom in Penn Station to be so disgusting that she would gag. She had expected knots of terrifying gang members to accost them. She had expected to be filled with fear and trembling.

Even the police were laughing, friendly-looking young men and women who resembled basketball or field-hockey coaches. They stood in pairs or trios, decorating street corners with their sharp uniforms, sauntering among the crowds.

Yellow taxis spun close to the sidewalk. They slid down an endlessly refilled row, like marbles spurting from a toy . . .

Stephen and Jodie stood outside Penn Station for several minutes, mesmerized, trying to adjust their thinking. Stephen said, "How many people do you think we can see from here?"

Jodie shook her head. She was stunned by the number of human beings passing before her. "Several hundred?"

"And that's just on one corner," said Stephen. "How many corners are there in New York?"

"Let's walk all the way around Penn Station," said Jodie. "Get oriented." Get oriented to what? she thought. She had the soup-kitchen list in her purse, but if Hannah had any cash at all, finding Hannah where she ate was not going to be easy.

Cheap eating abounded. Just from where they stood, they could see McDonald's, Wendy's, Roy Rogers, David's Cookies, four sidewalk hot-dog vendors, three ice-cream vendors, and a Chinatown Express.

The laminated folding map of Manhattan went less than halfway down into her jeans pocket. Jodie did not want to look like a tourist so she didn't pull it out the rest of the way.

They circled. On the other side of the vast railroad station was the largest and most beautiful post office Jodie had ever seen or imagined. The steps leading up to its many doors and its splendid columns were a block across. Hundreds of people sat licking ice-cream cones, nodding to music in their earphones, dozing in the sun. The massive stone steps might have been their own front porches. Insofar as people were dressed at all in this heat, they were dressed well.

There were thousands and thousands of people just on these sidewalks! Jodie and Stephen were actually trying to identify *one* of them?

I won't lose heart, Jodie told herself. This will be like a term paper. One sentence at a time. The longest journey begins with a single step and so forth.

Stephen refused to be overwhelmed. He had set himself a task and he was going to execute it. He looked into the masses, instead of around or through them. At first his eyes saw only a crowd: a black, white, and yellow blur of humanity. They were strangely alike, as if he were seeing a school of fish.

You weren't supposed to meet people's eyes in

New York, you were supposed to be careful of staring. But nobody Stephen saw could care less. Nobody was bothering to look back at Stephen.

Slowly, among the hordes of ordinary and unthreatening people, he began to pick out others.

A bag lady of indeterminate race pushed her belongings in a cart, on top of which she had balanced a broken-legged plastic chair and a bag full of returnable bottles she was plucking out of garbage cans. At one garbage can, she reached right between the legs of a black man who had draped himself like a corpse over the wire mesh. His snores blended into the throbbing from dozens of radios passing by on people's shoulders. A tall, dramatic woman with remarkably high heels strode by, and as she passed, Stephen thought, That's a man! He would have given this some consideration except that as they waited to cross the next street, he stood next to an unshaven and filthy white person, from whose toothless gums hung long yellow strands of some terrible food or disease.

Stephen began to feel better. All was not well in New York after all. There were still street people and he could pick them out and Hannah would be among them.

They walked uptown toward the first soup kitchen on their list.

On the next two blocks they struggled for sidewalk space. Confusingly, they were being assaulted by plastic-wrapped prom dresses and bright shapeless garments that hurtled past on long metal racks. The men pushing these racks seemed to be on a very tight schedule. Definitely not the kind to move over for tourists. Stephen could not imagine what they were up to.

It seemed logical to turn down a side street to get out of the crush.

It was not.

Stephen knew immediately that New Yorkers steered clear of this street.

There were no moving masses of humanity, but there were crowds. Although perhaps the word gang was better. A knot of young men, thin and hostile, leaned against obscene graffiti painted on a long-gone store. Across the street from them, against an abandoned car—or at least, a car whose wheels were in the process of being removed—lounged another group. All male. Their T-shirts were shredded, as if to display their destructive tendencies, and their earrings were weapons: miniature knives and guns hung from their earlobes.

Stephen felt like a dog, posturing, hackles up. Mistake, he thought, this was a mistake. It was a zone of some kind—whether a war zone, a drug zone, or what, he did not know. He could not read the signals passing between the groups. For all he knew they were just out shopping. Should he stare them down, or pretend they were not there? Grab Jodie and run back where they'd been, or walk on as if he always walked here, and knew it well? But what would be on the next block? More? Worse?

Jodie, apparently noticing nothing, moved ahead in her pretty new jeans and her soft pink blouse. The men began grinning. One by one, they came off the walls and stepped out, like scavenger dogs forming a pack.

Jodie chose this instant to pull out the map and peer around the neighborhood, squinting, trying to read distant street signs. "Put the map away," Stephen breathed.

The young men smirked. Stephen tried to be nonchalant. He was furious with himself for being afraid. He was not sufficiently street smart to know if these were men he ought to be afraid of, but he knew very well they were men Jodie ought to be afraid of.

"The first soup kitchen is right around here somewhere," said his sister, surging ahead. Stephen was forced to follow behind his sister, and he knew perfectly well the knots of men were laughing at him. He flushed and was careful not to meet any eyes.

Nothing happened.

What had he expected to have happen? How much of the dread specter of New York was truth, and how much was nonsense? How much were those guys just doing their bit to uphold legend and how much were they truly a threat? Reeve, he thought, would know.

He didn't look back, so he never would. And Jodie was correct. The first soup kitchen was two blocks away.

It was early for lunch, but the kitchen was open. People were going in.

Jodie was satisfied. This was what she had expected to find at Penn Station: the dregs and disasters of humanity. This soup kitchen was not serving people who had lost their jobs in a recession and needed a speck of help for a few weeks. This soup kitchen was for people who would always need help, or who were beyond it.

As they crossed the street and came within reach of the doors, Jodie's heart and courage failed her.

This is real, she thought. These people are really hungry. These people didn't take a train in from New Jersey. They really and truly do not have bathrooms and showers and after-school snacks. We can't go in there, and gawk, and peer at them, and show them Hannah's photograph! We're rich New Jersey tourists, is what we are.

Sun baked the street.

Stench filled Jodie's nostrils. Urine, she thought, trying to imagine living where people used the sidewalks. Booze. Vomit. She thought of the beautiful Johnson house in Connecticut. Of Hannah, who could have lived there. Who had chosen squalor instead.

Jodie would have gone straight home, but Stephen simply entered the building. They joined the line. The room was just a room, full of tables, but the people were not just people.

Nobody shoved, but the line, like the city, was crowded and full of chaotic energy. Jodie felt pressed upon even though nobody touched her, and encroached upon even though nobody looked at her. She was afraid of every single person in the room. Not one of them could possibly have a life she understood. Not one of them could ever have been at high school, worrying about friends and popularity and final grades.

Nobody said why were they there, or what were

their names. A woman heaved noodle-y soup into their bowls as if she were shoveling a garden. She was very squat, with hundreds of warts. Jodie fought back a shudder when she took her bowl. She studied her soup. It was thick, but with what?

Stephen murmured in Jodie's ear, "We don't have to ask half of them, anyway."

"Why not?"

"The black half aren't Hannah."

Jodie nodded seriously. "Got it."

It was a relief to sit and have only eight people next to her instead of hundreds. The table became a little tiny neighborhood, their own. She stirred her soup and felt oddly comfortable.

Stephen took out his photograph of Hannah. "We're looking for this woman," he said to their lunch companions. He was faintly surprised to be using English. These people were so different he felt as if he should speak some other tongue. "She was in New York two years ago. Have you seen her?"

They regarded Stephen with narrow, unblinking eyes. Finally one man said suspiciously, "Why you want her?"

They were on Hannah's side! It had never occurred to Stephen that people might see *him*, and not Hannah, as the bad guy. If he said, She's a kidnapper, we want to make her pay, they'd *really* be on Hannah's side. He heard himself lie. What he actually said out loud was, "She's my sister."

How weird, he thought, that I even thought of that. But in a way, she is my sister. Because she's sort of Janie's sister, and Janie is definitely my sister.

There was nothing to be heard except the intake of soup.

Noodles sloshed into hungry mouths.

The woman on Jodie's left said, "Pretty girl like that, if she wanted to go home, she'd go home. Maybe you better leave it alone. Pretty girl like that, maybe you doan wanna know what's she doin' now." Her voice was kind and sad. She was white, or would have been with a bath. Jodie breathed through her mouth.

"It's an old picture," said Stephen. "She's in her thirties now. I don't think she's pretty anymore."

"They doan stay pretty very long," agreed the woman. She smiled. Her mouth was full of gold teeth. One bore a silver star. "She a junkie by now," said the woman with satisfaction. "Like me. How ole you think I am?"

Jodie thought she was a hundred. Maybe an old-looking ninety.

"Thirty-six," said the woman.

Jodie's face fell apart, her jaw sagging, her eyes widening. She stared so intensely and so long it became an invasion. She could feel the woman getting hostile, but she could not stop. *This woman is thirty-six? This hag? Then Hannah? What will she look like after all this time?*

Jodie was too swamped in her thoughts to make another move, but Stephen gathered his courage and circled among the tables, showing his photograph, asking if they had seen his sister, who was older now, and probably not so pretty.

People seemed willing to look at the picture. But few spoke even a single syllable and most did not so much as shake their heads. They just waited for him to move on.

When he got back to Jodie, a new set of people were eating around her and she was sitting straight and tight and terrified among them. He and Jodie cleared their places, careful to do exactly what everybody else did. Neither of them had eaten a thing. He had to pour a full bowl of soup into the garbage. The attendant glared at Stephen from under sagging lids, for the crime of discarding food that others needed. But the man said nothing. That seemed to be the main rule of etiquette here. Say nothing.

For a moment they were afraid to leave. The dining hall was a safety zone, where they would be spared. But outside, on the hot sidewalks, among the hostile young men . . .

They left anyway, and again nothing happened.

They followed a short block back to Eighth Avenue, then Seventh. Here the men were wearing suits, not torn T-shirts. Subdued ties, not skull earrings. The streets here had half the energy and twice the safety.

Jodie felt calm enough to study the map again, working out the route to the next soup kitchen.

Stephen was counting human beings. He was trying to estimate the sheer volume of bodies they were seeing. He could not. It was unfathomable, how many people were out at noon in the summer sun.

They were looking for only one.

One.

Stephen's resident rage attacked him again. For

a moment he was one with the hostile unemployed men leaning against the storefronts.

Hannah has defeated us again! Hannah always wins. She always will. This is pointless. We were fools to think about it for a minute, let alone come into the city and try.

What a child he had been, thinking that he—Stephen the Bold, Stephen the Strong—would find Hannah, the Evil Kidnapper.

Stephen felt young, and there was nothing he hated more.

They went into another soup kitchen, this one part of a church. St. Somebody that Stephen was not sure how to pronounce. These people were less derelict, if there was such a description, but more sullen. Nobody could identify the photograph.

The third kitchen was so skanky they could not make themselves cross the street and get near. By the time they reached the fourth on their list, it had closed until supper. Hanging around were people with nowhere to go. Nobody among them would even look at the photograph. Most of them would not even look at Stephen. They seemed in a stupor. From the heat, perhaps. Or drugs. Or the unending defeats of life.

Jodie and Stephen wandered.

They found themselves in front of the public library, which they recognized by the famous stone lions. It too had vast steps on which hundreds of people rested. They bought ice cream and sat high up on the steps, gazing out at New York.

Building-wise, Jodie could not see much. People-wise, she felt that at least one million of New

York's many million had walked by. She was close to tears. It was hard to swallow the ice cream, and it melted on her and she didn't have a napkin and had to lick her hand.

To Stephen, Forty-second Street was full, not of potential Hannahs, but of successful businessmen in fine suits, who knew what they were doing, whose days were not stupid and futile, who would laugh if they knew what grandiose plans Stephen had brought with him on the train that morning.

Give it up, thought Stephen drearily.

And yet . . . against all odds . . . a little girl two states away had picked up a milk carton she normally would not touch, seen an old picture that nobody could recognize . . . and she had recognized it.

Against all odds . . .

Would they find Hannah against all odds?

He thought of all the hopeful young actors and actresses who came from their high-school plays to make it in New York; who must, like him, be shocked and scared by the city and the odds. But the odds were this: the ones who gave up and went home could never make it. The ones who trudged on just might.

Friday afternoon on a holiday weekend. Commuters were heading home early. Offices emptied as if the hands of God had turned the skyscrapers upside down and shaken out another zillion.

Fortified by the ice cream, they followed the laminated map to the next soup kitchen.

Stephen felt as if other humans had breathed in the available oxygen, leaving him gasping for air.

They took up the available sidewalk, shouldering him against pillars and building projects. But they didn't, really. Nobody touched him. Like the school of fish he had first thought they were, they slipped around him. Irritably. He was always swimming the wrong way.

They accomplished nothing at the next soup kitchen, and never located the shelter supposedly near it.

Stephen no longer cared whether they were in safe neighborhoods. He didn't care what color or what disease or what clothes anybody had. He just wanted to get home without anybody finding out what a jerk he was.

"Check the train schedule," he said to Jodie. "When's the next one?"

Jodie was not there.

He looked back, through the sweating, hurrying crowds.

She was gone.

His heart lurched, as his mother's had before him, twelve years before, when another Spring child vanished in the crowd.

Never to be seen again.

23

Stephen hunted for Jodie. His heart pounded so hard his ribs hurt. What will I say to Mom and Dad? he thought. How can this happen to us twice?

Where is she?

I have to find her!

The people of New York tightened in a hideous, evil net, impenetrable, and permanent. He could not break through, or see among them. He had thought he could pick Jodie out anywhere with her shining cap of red hair, but suddenly the world was full of redheads, and extremely full of people tall enough and wide enough to block Stephen's view of anything.

Jodie!

He found himself losing his mind, becoming disoriented and shocky. He ran to one corner, crossed the street, and crossed right back on the same street.

Every legendary nightmare on which he had been brought up—the trunks of six abandoned cars —the twirling soda-fountain seat on which his baby sister had last sat—filled his mind and exploded.

No, no, no, no, no, no, no, he thought. Not again! Not Jodie!

His arm was caught by somebody's hand and he was jerking free, ready to scream, I'm busy! Don't get in my way! when he saw that it was a policewoman. Pleasant-looking but calculating, estimating his potential for trouble the way Stephen would estimate the answer to a math problem.

"Something wrong?" she said politely.

"My sister." It was all he could manage. Explanations would be so long and involved that there was no point even starting. "I've lost my sister."

The policewoman just nodded. She did not let go of his arm.

Another voice said, "How old is she? She have red hair like yours?"

Stephen's turn to nod.

The other voice belonged to a policeman, thin, Hispanic, full of amusement. The cop pointed across the street. There was Jodie, talking with many gestures to another policeman on the opposite corner.

Stephen's terror turned abruptly into humiliation and a wave of scarlet shame completely enfolded him. The two cops next to him were laughing. He was a hick, a rube, a tourist.

"Walk light's on," said the policewoman, giving him a push into the street.

Stephen was so embarrassed he would not have minded being hit by a truck. But of course no truck hit him, and he reached Jodie, and now he was raging again, because his stupid worthless sister had left his side. It was her fault he had behaved so piti-

192

fully. Stephen was careful to keep his back turned to his pair of police.

Jodie's cop was a black man, built extremely wide, as if his shoulders had come from some other mold entirely than Stephen's. His skin seemed more solid than white skin would; in fact, his entire body seemed more solid. His muscles went all the way through.

Jodie was discussing soup kitchens with him. She had the rest of the list, places far enough way that they needed to take subways. The cop did not seem to be impressed with Jodie's plan of attack.

"Not neighborhoods for you two," said the cop firmly. "Stupid idea. Your parents know you're doing this?"

Stephen lied. "Sure they do."

The cop knew a lie when he heard one. "Sure they don't," he said, grinning. "Catch a train, kids. Go home."

"You don't understand," said Jodie, frowning. "My sister was kidnapped." Jodie, incredibly, was prepared for this discussion. She had a flattened milk carton with her, which she showed to the cop. Stephen had not known Jodie possessed one, let alone that she had brought it.

The cop glanced at the picture of Jennie Spring, age three. Stephen knew he had never seen it before. He knew immediately that among all the hype he'd heard in his life, it was hype from Mr. Mollison that New York police were hunting Hannah down. New York police did not know the first thing about the Jennie Spring case.

"You're looking for Jennie?" said the cop.

193

"No. Jennie is safe now. She's with—well, her other set of parents, so to speak. We're looking for the kidnapper." Jodie showed the photograph of Hannah to the policeman. "You've seen this," she informed him. "New York police are looking for her."

Just when Stephen thought he could not be more humiliated, he was more humiliated. Jodie sounded like Nancy Drew.

The cop rubbed his upper lip. "Mmm," he said, which was not very revealing. "And you two are hitting every soup kitchen in New York to locate this woman?" He looked at Stephen as if he had expected somebody Stephen's age to be more sensible. Stephen flushed.

"This calls for a Coke," said the cop. He handed a dollar to a vendor and popped open a can for himself. Stephen was low on funds. He bought one to share.

Jodie was encouraged by the presence of a police officer. She started so far back in the story of Jennie and Hannah that Stephen thought they would be here for days; that the policeman would have to bring in a second shift to hear the ending.

Stephen felt oddly insulated by the policeman, as if they were behind plate glass now, removed from the crush of the sidewalk, so it became a side-show instead.

The policeman seemed relatively young, and yet tired enough that he also seemed rather old. Stephen wanted to ask his age but couldn't think of a courteous way to do it. The cop asked no questions. He listened without expression. Surely even an experienced, jaded Manhattan cop was not used to stories like Hannah's.

When Jodie was done, he just said, "Still think the train home's a better idea."

Stephen remembered how much Jennie hated voices of authority getting all gentle on her.

"We can't go yet," said Jodie. "We're going to find Hannah. I want Hannah Javensen to pay. I *know* she's here. I *know* she is! If we go home now, we'll always wonder. Would Hannah have been around the next block? At the next shelter? I still want to get her!"

The cop tossed his empty can in the trash. He didn't seem like the kind of man who ever missed, and he didn't.

Jodie said, "Are you people actually looking for Hannah? I do not have the feeling that you are really looking."

The man's eyes revealed nothing. Stephen had no idea what he was thinking or expecting.

Fashionable businesswomen, kids on Rollerblades, derelicts shuffling, bikers making deliveries, tourists listening to guides went past like surfers on waves. And like the sea coming in, were endlessly replaced by more.

He thought of his parents in historic Williamsburg, with its charming colonial houses and sweet brick paths. What sidewalks could be more different?

"That's Hannah," said the cop softly, pointing.

Stephen's jaw fell.

Jodie whirled.

A figure swathed in layers of filthy clothing

stood in the gutter, picking up cigarette butts and examining them to see if there was anything left to smoke. It wore greenish pants, two cardigan sweaters, and a torn overcoat in spite of the heat. The hand not grubbing in refuse clung to the rim of a rusted shopping cart with a missing wheel. Plastic and paper bags filled the cart, and an old bowling-ball bag sat in the child's seat. A large pink plastic doll with no arms stuck out of the bowling bag.

The creature straightened up. Its hat had once been a baseball cap and the bill hung in ribbons over its face. Its fingers remained twisted, stuck permanently in a scavenging position.

Stephen would not even have known it was a woman. He saw no resemblance to the photograph of Hannah.

Jodie was staring like a two-year-old with her nose pressed up against the car window. This *thing* was the daughter of Frank and Miranda Javensen? "Arrest her!" said Jodie.

Stephen's mind cleared. There were loopholes here. "You don't know who that is," he accused the cop. "We told you about Hannah. You never heard that story before. You never saw that photograph before."

The policeman smiled without showing his teeth. It was more of a non-smile. It carried a deep understanding, the kind Stephen remembered from his grandmother.

"I don't know who that is," the cop agreed. He put a hand on Stephen's shoulder. It seemed too much weight for a hand. "But I know some things. When a person gets too old for a cult, when they can't bring in money, when they get sick, who needs 'em? Not the cult. Your sweet little girl from 1969? Your thoughtful college kid from 1972? Street people now. That's Hannah, even if we can't tell if it's a man or a woman. That's Hannah, even if she's a different race. Someday maybe we'll stumble over Hannah Javensen. Maybe we'll know it and maybe we won't. But you don't need to take revenge on Hannah. Life already has."

The cop's partner appeared. A woman. She tapped the radio strapped to her waist. "Come on." She jerked her head in the direction he was to come.

Jodie ignored this inconvenient interruption. "Do you think Mr. and Mrs. Johnson know?"

"Who are they, exactly?"

"They're the parents of Hannah and the ones who brought Jennie up."

"Oh, yeah. Yeah, they know what happened to Hannah. Why do you think they live in some pretty little Connecticut town in the middle of nowhere? Because they know. Why live in New York and see it, too?"

They know, thought Stephen. His heart, never before willing to enter the state of Connecticut, broke for the Johnsons. "Jennie went back to them," he said. He felt perilously close to tears. Crying would be the ultimate horror.

"Sounds okay to me," said the cop. "Everybody's happier than they were, even if they aren't completely happy."

Jodie put her arms around him and hugged him. She was a girl and did not mind when her tears spilled over. "Thank you for coming," she said, as if she had invited him to a party and would miss him once the festivities were over.

The woman cop rolled her eyes. "Can't leave you alone for a minute," she teased.

Their cop smiled again. Tight, kind of sad, kind of nice. "Don't worry about Hannah," he said. "She's beyond worry. Beyond punishment. Listen to me. You got a family that loves you, and Jennie's got a family that loves her. What else is there? Huh?"

The train was already at the platform, waiting.
They got on.
The train pulled out.
New York vanished behind them.
The train lurched past some stations and stopped at others.
"I'm glad we went in," said Stephen.
"Me, too."
"We found Hannah."
Jodie looked at him.
"Found her enough to count," said Stephen. "Found her enough to stop thinking about it."

The train went farther and farther south, closer and closer to home. By the time it reached their station, Stephen was a different person, almost as much as Jennie and Janie had been different people. His resident anger, his layers of hostility, were gone. He felt unusually peaceful.

He thought he really would go to visit Janie this summer. Get to know the Johnsons. And Reeve.

. . . Jodie stared out the train window at the thousands of occupied cars heading home for the long weekend. Thousands of houses would welcome them. So many strangers with so many sorrows.

But joy, too.

She would write to Janie after all. Like a sister. Maybe Janie would visit. If Reeve came, too, Janie wouldn't be afraid of the door shutting behind her and keeping her there. Maybe they would take the bed back down from the attic, so Janie could see she still had a place if she ever wanted it.

Stephen was right: they had found Hannah enough to count.

And the policeman, he was the most right of all.

You got a family that loves you, thought Jodie Spring, and Janie's got a family that loves her. What else is there?

ABOUT THE AUTHOR

CAROLINE B. COONEY is the author of many novels for young adults, including *Among Friends, The Girl Who Invented Romance, Camp Girl-Meets-Boy, Camp Reunion, Family Reunion, Don't Blame the Music,* an ALA Best Book for Young Adults, *The Face on the Milk Carton, Twenty Pageants Later,* and *Operation: Homefront.* She lives in Westbrook, Connecticut.

.